My Amish Roots

Nicola Meyer

Published by Trellis Publishing, 2021.

MY AMISH ROOTS

First edition. July 12, 2021.

ISBN: 979-8224549481

Written by Nicola Meyer.

My Amish Roots

Nicola Meyer

Chapter 1

Haylee lay in the darkness of her room staring out of the window at the moon that hung low in the sky, her only consort in her lonely life. Four years after meeting Jase, her heart was broken into a million pieces and scattered across the vast expanse of her own insignificant universe. Move on, they said, he's not worth it, they said, you deserve better. What did they know? None of her so called friends could ever imagine how she felt deep down and how utterly destroyed she was when she walked in on Jase in the arms of her best friend, Lucile. Of course the first thing both of them shouted when caught in the act was – it's not what you think!

After Jase pleaded with her and Lucile convinced her that it was an irresponsible judgement error on her part and that it would never happen again, she gave it another shot. She should have known better. Naïve little Haylee, who only tries to see the good in people ended up as the biggest fool of them all and when it happened a second time, she could no longer be ignorant. It was obvious that between the chemical combination of Lucile's raging pheromones and Jase's ego boosted testosterone, she never stood a chance. She had to finally admit to herself that she was never going to find true love, and friendships are feeble pastimes for pre-schoolers.

It's been almost two months since her relationship with Jase ended, and it wasn't long after that, that she also handed in her resignation as an article clerk. Breaking up with Jase and seeing him once in a blue moon she could handle well, but working with him and sharing the same open office day in and day out was a little too much to handle. It amazed her how men in could be so callous and move on without a worry in the world. She had managed thus far, but the more she sat at home she started to feel cooped up like a bird in a too small cage.

She sighed and tugged her blanket over her shoulders and tucked it under her chin as she turned onto her other side, this time staring at her graduation photo. She stood tall and proud, alone in her toga with her rolled up certificate in her hand, no immediate family to share her successes with her. Her adoptive mother had passed away six months short of her graduation that year. Haylee sniffed and blinked away the tears. She didn't cry then and she won't cry now. Finally giving up on sleeping she tossed the blanket back and sat up in bed. Her mom always told her, that every person has left something behind in their past, that sits there and waits until they go back to find it and resolve it. And until recently she had never thought she wanted to go back there. She was only four when she was adopted, a lonely gray mouse stuck in foster care. From the first day she arrived at her new family, she was accepted and spoiled rotten. She never needed for anything in her life, and she never felt as if she was any different to any of the other kids, so why she suddenly felt like digging out the past was a mystery to her, but every day it became more and more pressing. And here at two in the morning, she was stuck between forcing herself to sleep or logging into her email to see if the adoption agency managed to track down her biological mother or family. Insomnia won the battle and she finally made herself a cup of coffee and sat down at her desk and logged into her emails.

Dear Miss Jones

We have managed to track down your biological mother, but it is with regret that we inform you that she passed away a few years ago due to illness. We have however managed to track down her parents, your grandparents. We do however wish that you consider the fact that they may not...

Hayley stared at the email, reading it over and over again, somehow grief evaded her, and it was like reading the sad story of a stranger. What she did learn from this was that her mother was born Amish, and that her grandparents lived in an Amish community in Ethridge, Tennessee. But even if she knew who they were, what good would that do now? It wasn't as if she could reunite with her long lost mother anymore. But what she might be able to figure out is what type of woman her mother was and what type of life she lived. Maybe it will even shed some light on why her mother gave her up for adoption. As she spent her time reading up on the Amish and their culture, it became more and more evident that her mother may not have had a choice, but this was pure speculation. And unless she took the time to find these things out for herself, she would always be guessing about the woman who brought her into this world.

Besides, it wasn't as if she had anything better to do with her time. She had no job, no love life and no coffee, she thought as she looked at the empty canister in front of her.

That was it; she was going to take the last of her savings and head to Ethridge and find the Lapp's.

Chapter 2

The whole way to Ethridge, Hayley kept wondering if she was making a mistake. She was about to embark on a journey she was in the least bit prepared for. Before she left everything behind, she made effort to reinvent her wardrobe with a few modest outfits just so that she wouldn't look too outrageous amongst the Amish. But even now as she sat in the back of the cab, her heart was beating a million miles a second and she was on the verge of having a nervous breakdown. She had just left behind the only life she knew, not that there was much left of her for her to salvage, but she was somewhat comfortable where she was.

The cab pulled into the small town of Ethridge and stopped in front of what appeared to be a touring business.

"This is as far as I can go," the cab driver said and pointed to this meter.

Hayley nodded and fished for cash to pay the cab driver and the moment her bags were offloaded and she stood like a singled out deer in hunting season outside on the sidewalk she wanted to burst out in tears. Whatever was she thinking coming out here?

"Hello, may I help you?"

Startled Hayley nearly lost her balance as she spun to look at the stranger behind her, "Oh-I-um, well, I'm looking for someone," she said and dug in her purse, "Mr. and Mrs. Lapp?"

"Oh Fredrick and Mary Lapp, yah, they live here. I can take you," the young man said.

"You know them?" Hayley asked in disbelief.

"Yah, well it's a small community we all know each other," he said tucking his thumbs under his suspenders.

Hayley couldn't help but stare, wondering if all Amish men were this good looking. This guy couldn't be much older than her twenty-five. And although he was dressed modestly in what she had to assume Amish clothes, he looked reasonably attractive.He had ebony black hair with willow green eyes set deeply in his skull.

"If you're done staring..." he said interrupting her thoughts with his brows drawn together.

Embarrassingly she shook her head, "I'm so sorry, I just... it has been a really long day and I've traveled a long way."

"No matter, my name is Duncan," he said and nodded his head courteously, extending his hand.

"Hayley," she said and gave his hand an overly firm shake.

"Well I best be getting you to the Lapp's, the weather is turning foul."

Without notice he started loading her luggage into a carriage that stood nearby and then patted the back of the carriage, indicating her seat.

Who was she to ask questions, she hadn't the foggiest about their customs and every website she visited to learn about them were know-it-all windbags who have made up assumptions. So instead of opposing she hopped into the back of the carriage and sat down.

"So do you know the Lapps?" Duncan called over his shoulder as they made their way into the town.

"I...sort of, actually, I knew their daughter," she lied, she had no clue what their daughter was like. Just because Hannah Lapp gave birth to her, didn't exactly mean she knew her.

"I think you might have them mistaken for someone different, they only have a son, but Kendrick moved to Lancaster with his wife."

Well, this was a good start, she thought as she tucked her lip under her teeth, "Perhaps I am confused, but I suppose there is no harm in meeting them. Maybe they might know Hannah Lapp as extended family."

"Hannah Lapp," Duncan repeated, "The name sounds familiar."

The carriage came to a halt and Hayley fell forward along with her luggage and just then the heavens opened up.

"Come!" Duncan called and reached for a sheet to cover her luggage before effortlessly lifting her off the wagon and placing her on her feet, "The Lapp's live here. If you hurry I can wait and take you back to Richland Inn."

"Wait, what do you mean back to town, I need to be here in Ethridge," she protested as Duncan lead her up to the house where the Lapps lived.

"Well if the Lapps won't let you stay in their home, you have nowhere else to stay, unless you want to sleep in the barn."

"The barn?" she asked appalled.

"Duncan, vas in der velt?" an elderly man interrupted as he opened his door.

Duncan immediately removed his hat and clutched it in front of him then looked at her before turning his attention back to the older man.

"Mister Lapp, this is Hayley. She's come to Ethridge to look for..."

Before Duncan could continue Hayley stepped up and extended her hand, "Grandfather?"

The older man's complexion paled, and he exchanged looks with Duncan then looked at Hayley, "You're mistaken," he mumbled and moved to close the door, but then an elderly woman appeared and the expression on her face was one of pure shock.

"Hannah... you look just like her," she said in a trembling voice as her eyes shot full of tears.

"Grandmother?" Haylee said as she stood with her hands folded in front of her.

"Come, you're going to get soaking wet out in the rain," she said as she dragged Hayley into the house, despite her Grandfather's disapproval.

And as she disappeared into the kitchen she heard her grandfather mumble for Duncan to bring her luggage inside.

Her grandparents, she couldn't believe it. She was actually in the very house her biological mother grew up in. Her grandmother seemed far more accepting of her than her grandfather did, but she refused to make any assumptions until she had all the facts. For now, she will take the time she had to get to know them.

Chapter 3

A week since her arrival and all she could determine was that her mother, Hanna Lapp went on a Rumspringa and never returned.

"Did she never write to you?" Hayley asked her grandmother one morning after her grandfather left to go to work.

"She wrote to us, but only ever to let us know she was fine," her grandmother said softly as she continued with her sewing.

"But weren't you in the least bit worried?"

Mary put down her sewing and reached out for Hayley's hand, "Yah, we were worried, especially your grandfather, but our laws are different to those on the outside. Hannah made her choice and she had a chance to return."

Hayley sat quietly for a moment and squeezed her grandmother's hand. The short while she had been here in the Amish community of Ethridge, she had found a sense of peace and tranquillity she never felt before. With the exception of a minority of locals who walked wide circles around her, the younger people like her were friendly and very accommodating. She couldn't understand why her mother would have left for good, and trade this life for what lay outside in the world. But then, being on holiday in a strange place was far different that living the life in full.

A knock on the door drew her attention and her grandmother quickly set her sewing aside and went to open the door, and a few seconds later she returned with Duncan in tow.

"Hayley, Duncan is here to see you," her grandmother said smiling.

Duncan was another person she was growing fond of at an alarming rate, but thankfully the walls she erected around herself kept her level headed. She knew that the only reason she felt closer to him than any of the others was that he was the first person she met when she arrived.

"Hi Duncan, what a nice surprise," she said standing up.

"Good day to you Hayley," he nodded tucking his thumbs in his suspenders, "I was wondering if you would like to go to the market today, I have a few errands to run."

Hayley felt the slight flutter of butterflies in her stomach and tugged her hand into her midriff. It would be rather nice to get out a little and get to know other parts of the community, she thought and then nodded.

"It would be lovely, let me get my coat and purse," she said and hurried to her room.

She forced herself not to eavesdrop on her grandmother' and Duncan's conversation and quickly got what she needed before joining them.

In no time they were on the carriage and on their way to the market, this time Hayley got to sit in the front and not like some baggage on the back.

"So how are you enjoying your stay here in Ethridge?" Duncan asked curiously.

"It's nice. I mean, it's very different to city life, but so far I'm enjoying the peace and quiet," she said and glanced out over the landscape.

"Yah, it's very quiet. So did you manage to find out about Hannah?"

"A little," she said.

She didn't want to put the Lapps in any sort of disrepute, but she found it hard to believe that Duncan had no clue about her, but then again, he was probably still a baby when Hannah left the Amish community.

"So will you be moving on then?" he said clearing his throat.

Hayley turned to look at him and smiled, "Not sure, maybe. Tell me about this Rumspringa thing."

Duncan laughed and looked at her, "Well, Rumspringa means to run around, when the youngsters turn sixteen they can choose to go out and experience things outside of our community. It's each one's choice, some do it and some don't."

"Did you ever, I mean did you do it when you turned sixteen?" she asked curiously.

"Nay, I never did. I have all I need right here."

"So you never wonder what lies out in the cities."

Duncan drew the carriage to a halt and then turned to look at Hayley, studying her with those intense willow green eyes.

"Most young men leave because they are not satisfied with their life here, mostly because they are tempted by the modern world, and women," he said, his cheeks growing rosy.

Hayley tried to hide her smile and coughed softly, "So you never wanted to go find some hanky-panky?"

"Hanky -panky?" Duncan asked and blinked, "What is that?"

"Uh... well meeting women, dating and so on."

Duncan threw his head back and laughed, "Oh no, I had no interest in those things. Not then anyway," he said and then tugged on the reins sending the horse back onto the road, "I always believed that at the right time God will send the right woman my way. I'm a patient man Hayley Jones."

When he looked at her then, she felt her heart flutter in her chest and she immediately looked the other way. Her mind was clearly playing tricks on her; there was no way that Duncan would even consider looking at her twice. She was an outsider for one, and secondly, she wasn't exactly a virgin either. And although she still knew very little about their laws and traditions, she was sure the Amish probably had the highest moral values in the world second to nuns.

The rest of their trip was in silence, and a few miles further they finally reached the Amish Country Mall. Hayley was quite surprised by the variety of goods that were sold at this place, but more so how many non-Amish visited the place. It was a tourist distraction for curious people. And as she stood next to Duncan and the Carriage in her own authentic Amish dress, a sense of pride washed over her. Surprised that she actually felt Amish in some far-fetched way, she smiled at Duncan and then headed into the shop. She found it quite amusing that it was called a Mall when all it really had were old antique trinkets and a limited menu of food. There were some items for sale but it was hardly considered anything close to a shopping mall. When she exited the store she found Duncan standing next to her grandfather, both in deep conversation. Instead of barging in on them she took a walk around the store to give them their own time. Her grandfather had hardly spoken a word to her since her arrival and he was still a great big mystery to her. On occasion when she did ask her gran about him, she simply avoided the topic. She wasn't any closer to find out exactly why her mother never came back.

Chapter 4

Duncan couldn't help but admire Hayley, and although she was an outsider, she seemed to adapt quite well to the Amish life. It's been two weeks since he met her, and the more time he spent with her the more he started to like her. The first day he saw her was the first time he ever really looked at a woman. She was modestly dressed in a floral print dress that flowed elegantly down her body to her calves, but what intrigued him most was her shyness. The fact that he had the impulsive need to run his fingers through her long brown tresses was abnormal for him and he quickly stifled that need, by reminding himself that she was an outsider, which helped.

Normally when outsiders visited the Amish communities they stuck to their modern clothes, where the women wore as little as possible. No wonder so many of the Amish boys opted to go on their expedition to the cities, being tempted by the promises that the modern world presented. Two of his own best friends went out to experience the world and all it had to offer, but he never felt that desire or pull to know what happens out there. He was more than content to live this life of simplicity, working on the farm and making goat's cheese. There were many times when he attended the sings and where he contemplated the option of taking a wife, but none of the girls here in Ethridge ever made him feel the way he did now. And he was adamant that if he was going to take a wife, it would be someone who would completely consume his thoughts. He wanted the same love with a wife than his mother and father shared. He had never seen them argue, and they always showed their affection towards each other. And if they could have such a devoted marriage, why could he not have the same?

Duncan was caught in his own thoughts when the smell of burning wood and grass wafted through the air.

"Duncan!" It was Hayley who rode towards him on one of the Lapp's horses, her eyes wide, "Come quick, my grandfather's barn is on fire!" she cried.

In an instant, Duncan had called his father and his neighbors, and everyone else he could alert and they were on their way by carriage to the Lapp's farmlands. Up ahead he could see the plume of fire explode into the gray sky. Flames rolled outwards and embers were flying up into the sky.

When he pulled up next to Hayley where she dismounted the horse, he took the reins and handed it to another young man, "Take the horse to my father's barn and keep it there," he instructed and then turned to Hayley, "What happened?"

"I have no idea, we were all having dinner when we heard the loud crash of lightning, and not long after that the smoke was everywhere," she said ringing her hands together.

Duncan's concern for Hayley had to be set aside, and although he wanted to comfort her, he had to attend to the bigger problem.

"Okay, go to the house and stay inside," he ordered as he scooped a bucket of water from the trough.

"But I can help," she protested and reached for a small barrel.

"You've done enough, now go and sit with your grandmother, I'm sure she could use the company."

Her mouth opened in protest but then shut, and with a slight nod, she ran across the field towards the house.

They fought all night to get the fire under control, thankfully the Lord had blessed them with rain to help put the fire out, but all that was left were the charred remains of the barn in the smoky morning air that reeked of burnt wood and straw. His father had warned Fredrick about the tall dead tree that stood so close to the barn. But misfortune led to lighting striking the dead tree and causing it to fall on to the barn. Luckily it was only the barn that burned down, somehow the horses were freed before the barn was completely on fire, and he has the slightest suspicion that it was Hayley's quick thinking that saved the animals. As for the equipment, it was all replaceable.

"Thank you, son, if you didn't arrive when you did I would have lost all my horses," Mr. Lapp said as he came to stand next to Duncan.

"Nay, that was not my doing. Hayley saved the horses," he said and looked at the older man.

"Hayley saved them?" he asked disbelievingly.

"Yah, she came to fetch me on horseback, I've never seen a woman ride so well, but she came to call me straight away. By the time I got here the horses were already in the fields and Kent took them to my barn."

Fredrick stood quietly for a while rubbing his chin, and Duncan knew that he had his own demons to face. He too had never heard of Hannah Lapp, but spending time with Hayley he had learned a great deal.

"She's seeking your approval," Duncan said crossing his arms as both of them looked at what remained of the barn, "She deserves a fair chance."

"You're right," Fredrick said and then headed towards the house.

Duncan looked as the older man walked away, his shoulders hunched as if he carried a heavy burden, but he knew Hayley deserved a fair chance, she had nothing to do with her mother's disobedience or her choice to give her up for adoption.

Later that day, Duncan stood in his father's barn, grooming the Lapps' horses. The least he could do was make sure that none of them were injured. But more than anything he needed to keep busy so that he could chase the thoughts of Hayley from his mind. Every waking hour was seemingly consumed by thoughts of her, and after her courageous act it was even worse. Now he knew exactly how King Solomon must have felt, being tempted by a beautiful woman.

"Duncan?" he heard Hayley's voice from outside the barn.

"In here!" he answered and tossed the brush in the sack hanging on the wall.

"Oh there you are," she said smiling and held out a basket for him, "Grandma and I baked these to thank you for helping us out with the horses."

Duncan smiled and took the basket filled with cookies, "Thanks, but I think you deserve all the credit, if it wasn't for you these horses would be charred with the barn."

He noticed Hayley blush as she averted her eyes, "I love horses, I had to do something."

Duncan stepped closer and reached out to tuck his finger under her chin, "And you did an amazing job of saving them," he said but his voice betrayed him.

This close to her, he could smell the fresh scent of lavender and vanilla, and although it was just the crook of his finger brushing her unblemished skin under her chin, it was the silk soft smoothness that tempted him more than anything. And without a second thought, he stepped in and pressed his lips against hers. Hers were soft, like cotton pillows and although the kiss was brief, it was a defying moment for him. He knew there and then that Hayley was the woman he'd been waiting for all these years.

He broke the chaste kiss but didn't step away from her; instead he kept his eyes locked on hers. It was that moment between two people where words were irrelevant syllables and consonants were fleeting sounds that would never be able to express the emotions that sparked between them.

It was Hayley that stepped away first, and how shyly tucked a strand of hair behind her ear.

"My grandfather said that they will be doing a barn rising this coming weekend, will you come?" she asked softly.

"I wouldn't miss it for the world," Duncan said.

And as Hayley walked back out of the Barn she looked back over at him again and smiled.

Duncan felt like a teenager for the first time, and now more than ever was he determined to make Hayley Jones his wife.

Chapter 5

The barn raising was well on its way, the men from the community had spent most of the morning working and Hayley was amazed by how quickly the barn started taking shape. She heard many stories about this experience and how the Amish are able to build an entire barn in one day, but she had never seen it with her own eyes. Duncan was at the front line of everything. He did the planning and the design, his skill as a builder came in handy and it appeared that young to old admired him, but not nearly as much as she did.

When she first decided to come to Ethridge, finding love was the last thing she anticipated. After her failed engagement to Jase, she had sworn off on ever dating again, but here she was, utterly captivated by Duncan. He was the complete opposite to Jase. He was kind, considerate, a true gentleman and there was something about him that she craved.

"He's a fine young man," her gran said as she handed her the basket of fresh fruit.

Hayley tore her eyes away from the barn and smiled at her gran, "Yes, he is," she admitted.

"You know, Hannah never told us about you until after she gave you up for adoption," her grandmother started, "When she told us your grandfather begged her to withdraw the adoption and rather send you to us."

Hayley sat down opposite her gran at the wooden table, "So you did know about me?"

"Oh yes we did, but your mother had already handed you to your new parents, and we had no way of finding you. That day you arrived here in Ethridge, you were a spitting image of my Hannah."

Hayley's eyes shot full of tears and she reached out to take her grandmother's hand, "My adopted parents were good people, they really looked after me as if I was their own."

"I know, but I can't help wonder just how things would have been if Hannah had come back home," the older woman admitted and lowered her eyes.

"I'm here now though, and you've made me feel at home."

"Yah, yah, I know. I've been trying my best. Your grandfather blames himself for what happened, but he's a good man."

Hayley smiled and then looked back at the men toiling in the sun. Her grandfather was a proud but humble man, and she knew that deep down he cared for her.

By six o'clock that evening, the barn stood tall in all its glory. Brand spanking new as if no disaster had struck it just a week ago, and everyone in the community had gathered to celebrate the event. It was a festive atmosphere and for the first time in her life Hayley felt as if she belonged. Over the weeks she spent here in Ethridge learning to bake and quilt, she hardly thought of her life in the city. And the hustle and bustle of peak hour traffic and busy shopping malls were nothing but a distant memory of a temporary life she once knew.

She made a few friends and even the older people had started to like her. Maybe it was due to the fact that she did not come here to dispute their faith or their ways, but she embraced it like any Amish citizen would.

From across the group of people, she caught Duncan looking at her. But instead of looking away, she smiled at him, and even when one of his friends tapped him on his shoulder he still looked her way, refusing to drop his glance. The sight of him made her knees weak. She had to force herself to look away before her grandfather came to sit beside her.

"My dear," he started sounding uncomfortable, "I owe you an apology for my behavior."

Hayley turned to her grandfather and smiled, "No need, you had a lot to cope with, with my untimely arrival. I should have taken better care to notify you before I just dropped in."

"No, it's not that. I-I never gave your mother a chance to rectify things and for that, I am forever guilty, I should have gone to find her."

Fredrick pinched the bridge of his nose and shut his eyes and Hayley knew he was fighting back the tears, she gently placed her hand on his, "The choices we make are our own, and we are all responsible for them, no one can take responsibility for the mistakes of others."

There was a moment of silence, and when her grandfather looked up at her again he smiled tenderly, "You will make a wonderful Amish woman," he said and patted her hand, "And Duncan would choose well to ask for your hand."

"Hayley, come!" One of the girls called and tugged her up by her hand, "You must join in on the sing."

Before Hayley could process the words of her grandfather she was caught smack bang in the middle with a bunch of the younger people, and although there were no instruments, the clapping of hands and the harmonies of voices made the songs come to life. Among the crowd was Duncan, subtly making his way closer to her and the closer he came the more her heart beat out of control and the butterflies that hijacked her insides fluttered up a storm. She might very well be an outsider but she could not deny the fact that somehow Providence had claimed a victory.

"Would you spare me a few minutes of your time?" Duncan whispered as he reached her.

"Of course," she said and followed him outside.

Duncan had his hands tucked in his pockets as he stood outside. The moonlight spilled down from the heavens like a silver curtain, bathing their surroundings in silver dust and casting its subtle glow over them. And as Hayley came to stand next to him, they both glanced up at the sky.

"Hayley..."

"Duncan..."

They started at the same time and then burst out laughing.

"You first," Hayley insisted and Duncan smiled and turned towards her.

"Okay, well, I'm sure this will come as no surprise to you, but I thought it best I clear the air," he started clutching his hand in his hands, "I think or rather, I know that I have grown very fond of you, and I know that it may be a little more complicated than usual, but I have spoken to your grandfather."

Hayley stood playing with the string of her prayer cap, coiling it around her index finger nervously. It felt as if her heart was going to jump out of her throat as Duncan went on, explaining how he had asked her grandfather if he would allow him to court her. A few weeks ago, she would never have considered this, but now where she stood under the moonlit sky, with her hand in Duncan's she knew exactly what she wanted.

"And did my grandfather approve?" she asked curiously biting her lip.

"He did indeed, which is why I have gathered to courage to ask you in person," he admitted and smiled.

Hayley shifted her weight and sucked in a breath, she had no idea how Amish dating customs worked. Of all the things she had yet to learn, dating hardly featured and she recalled only briefly spot reading over that section.

"So are we going to be bundling?" she asked innocently and blushed.

Duncan raised his brows and chuckled, "My dear Hayley, you have so much to learn still, no one does that anymore," he said and stepped closer to her and reached to remove her prayer cap.

"Is that allowed?" She whispered softly as Duncan's lips hovered over hers and he pulled the pin that secured her hair in a bun lose.

"What happens between us, and the Lord, is all that matters," he said and then wrapped her loose braid around his hand and kissed her fully on the lips.

Chapter 6

Hayley stood in front of the mirror, while her grandmother fussed with her long hair. It's been a year since she joined the community and although her and Duncan's feelings for each other were no secret to the rest of the community, they both kept their word to follow the rules and customs as required by the Amish Council.

"So the food is almost ready. Once your Grandfather and I are off to the church service, you and Duncan can sit down and celebrate your betrothal."

Hayley looked in the reflection of the mirror at her grandmother, the woman she had grown to love and smiled, "Do you think I will make him happy, Grossmammi?" she asked.

"Natuurlijk! You're his future and the woman he had been waiting for all this time," her gran reassured her.

After her grandparents left to go to church, where the minister would be announcing the brides to be, she waited patiently at the house for Duncan to arrive. She kept looking at the clock on the wall, it was a unique hand crafted clock made especially for her by Duncan, as a courtship gift. Time seemed like it had deliberately slowed down, and when she heard the carriage finally pull up in front of the house, she had to force herself to stay calm and not rush into his arms. Other than the first time he kissed her, and the second and the third, this was probably one of the most amazing moments in her life. After tonight, she would officially be engaged, and by October, only two months away, she would be Mrs. Hayley Beiler.

"You do know that you still have a choice right?" Duncan said much later after they had finished dessert.

"I have made my choice, and it is to stay here with you," she said smiling.

They were seated on a wooden bench outside on the porch; waiting for the Lapp's to arrive.

"Are you a hundred percent sure?" he asked again, this time lacing his fingers with hers.

Hayley turned to him and placed her free hand over their entwined fingers. The past few months she had made the effort to learn their various customs, do bible study, get familiar with their laws, but she knew beyond anything that her life was here with him.

"Duncan, I am happy and I would not change this for anything," she said and then leaned close enough for her lips to brush his, "Ich liebe dich," she whispered and gave him a chaste kiss on his lips.

"And I love you, Hayley Jones," Duncan said, smiling from ear to ear and then quoted Songs of Solomon, "You are altogether beautiful, my darling, beautiful in every way."

~*~

Most of all, let love guide your way. Col 3:14

The Chosen Amish

Deidra Scott

Chapter One

David Miller took a deep breath of the clean spring morning air and sighed. Spring...it had always been the promise of fresh starts and new beginnings.

Not that there was very much hope of a new beginning for him.

Reaching up to adjust his straw hat on his head, David kicked at a clump of dirt in the midst of his freshly plowed corn field. He started toward the house where his wife, Ida, would surely be up making breakfast. Soon it would be time to get the horses hitched up and start on their way to church.

"*Daed, Daed*!" The voice of his six-year-old son, Lucas made David look up and give a slight smile in the child's direction. The little boy was running through the clumps of dirt, struggling to keep his footing. There were few things in life that made David quite as happy as the sight of his little boy. The spitting image of David with his curly dark hair and brown eyes, Lucas certainly made his father proud.

Reaching down, David scooped the little boy up in his arms right before he could trip over a clump of dirt.

"Watch it there, son," David warned him as he slung the child under his arm like a sack of potatoes, "No need to get your church clothes all filthy."

Lucas giggled as he bounced in his father's arms.

"*Mamm* said to tell you it's almost time to leave!" Lucas informed David when he finally reached the yard and had put him back on his feet in the soft grass, "She said you'd better get yourself ready or we'd be late again."

David sucked in a deep breath and slowly shook his head. *Ach*, if that woman didn't nag him about everything. And lately it seemed that she was trying to use his child to nag him as well!

"You tell your *Mamm*..." David's voice trailed off as he thought better of his words. Letting out a huff, he gave Lucas a push toward the house, "Tell her I'll be in soon. I just want to go on and hitch up the buggy."

Walking toward the barn, David wished that he could just hole himself away in it for good. It was starting to look like life with his wife just wasn't worth living.

By the time David had the horses ready and went into the house, it was easy to tell that Ida was in a tizzy.

"David!" Ida exclaimed as she glanced at the pocket watch lying on the table, "Do you realize how late it is? *Ach*! We should have been on the road fifteen minutes ago!"

"We will get there," David assured her as he reached out for his black felt hat.

When he reached for it, Ida let out a deep groan and hurried to his side, "David, look at your shirt! You've got dirt all over the sleeve. Why did you wear it to go out into the fields, anyway?"

David felt like he was a bottle of soda pop that had been shaken for too long and was finally being released to explode. Unable to hold in his fury any longer, he turned on his heels and looked at his wife in surprise, "Can't I do anything good enough for you?!" .

Obviously taken back by his outburst, Ida took a deep breath and stepped away to make room between them.

"Let's just get going," She managed to whisper as she reached for her black bonnet.

Sitting on the hard wooden church pew, David tried to keep his mind on the service, but it seemed that his thoughts were constantly traveling to any other topic.

Realizing the sermon was coming to a close, David sat up straighter, anxious to get out of the packed Amish house and back to his own home.

"Before we enjoy the delicious meal that the Millers have prepared, I have an exciting announcement," Preached Ben said. Motioning toward someone in the crowd, David turned and let his eyes follow a young Amish couple as they slowly rose to their feet.

"Joe Eicher and Miriam Kiem want to announce their engagement," Preacher Ben continued.

David watched the young couple glance at each other, their eyes filling with excitement and love.

It had been a long time since Ida and David had looked at each other like that.

There had been a time when David had truly thought that he loved Ida. He could still remember their first encounter. He had been attending a wedding for his cousin in Indiana and had managed to come across the spunky sixteen-year-old girl. She was so cheerful, her round cheeks so rosy, and she had such a happy skip to her step. Just being around Ida had made David happy...so happy that he could hardly stand to come back home to Kentucky. *Ach*, how he'd worried that she would find another beau before he had a chance to get to know her!

But now...well, everything had changed now. Maybe it had simply been too many years together...maybe time was dragging them apart as they each became more consumed with their own chores and daily tasks. Whatever the case, David had to admit that he no longer felt anything close to love when he saw his wife; in fact, more days then not, he found himself battling feelings that bordered closer to outright dislike.

"David? David!" Ida's voice brought David out of his thoughts, alerting him that church services were over and he was the only one still sitting on a bench.

Pulling himself to his feet, David tried to ignore the irritation that he sensed in his wife's voice.

"Where's Lucas?" David asked as he reached for his black felt hat.

"He's out in the barn playing with some of his friends before we eat." Ida sounded so cheerful that her syrupy words made David want to vomit. Why was she putting on a show, acting like she liked him? David knew the truth and he was sick of watching his wife put on a good front in public.

David grimaced and shook his head, "I don't feel *gut*. I think we need to just go on home."

Ida opened her mouth to protest but then seemed to stop herself. Lifting her hand, she placed it on his forehead. "You don't feel hot," she announced, "Maybe you just need to eat."

Reaching up, David grabbed her hand in his grip and jerked it away from his face.

"I think I know when I feel sick," he snarled, tightening his grasp. Ida looked up to meet his stare, her blue eyes suddenly huge and filling with tears.

Releasing his grasp with a force that almost made her lose her balance, David looked away and stated, "Get Lucas. I'll be in the buggy."

Chapter Two

As David went out to the barn to unhitch his horse from the buggy, he found himself struggling with an assortment of feelings. Ida hadn't spoken a word the entire ride home. Lucas, who had wanted to stay and eat with the rest of the Amish community, had spent the trip crying.

Running a hand through his hair, David shook his head in frustration. It seemed like everything was becoming too stressful to ever hope to handle.

Taking a deep breath, David released the horse into a stall and closed the gate behind it. Turning around, David made his way to a feed trough and lifted the wooden lid. Reaching deep down into the recess of the empty storage bin, he gave a sigh of relief when he pulled up the bottle of whiskey that had been hidden from sight.

For some reason, he was always afraid that Ida would have found it and taken it away.

Uncorking the bottle, David lifted it to his lips and took a swig before he set the bottle aside and started hanging the bridle, bits, and other pieces of buggy equipment on their places in the barn.

David had always drunk a little bit. When he was younger, it hadn't seemed like such a big deal. Although he knew his parents did not like it, living in a very relaxed Amish community, the young folks were allowed to bring alcohol to their gatherings if they wanted. David had never thought a thing of trying a little bit every now and again. Something about it simply seemed to make the gatherings more enjoyable...and, as time passed, David started to realize that alcohol made everything in life a little more enjoyable.

It still did.

"David?" The voice of his wife made David jump and nearly spill the whiskey across the front of his white shirt. Letting out a low curse, David acted quickly and hid the bottle on a nearby shelf that was full of tools.

"David?" Ida called out again.

"I'm back here," David managed to call out, hoping that his secret was safely out of sight.

Taking a deep breath, David looked up to see his wife making her way toward him. David could feel his heart beating wildly in his chest and his hands shaking at his side. His legs felt so wobbly, he wondered if he could continue to stand without sinking to the ground in a pile.

"*Ach*, I was starting to wonder if you'd just vanished!" Ida announced with a forced laugh as she stopped in front of him.

"Nope." David tried to sound nonchalant as he hung up a bridle and turned to look at her. He bit his tongue to keep from adding, *I'm sure you wish I would*!

Coming to his side, Ida reached out awkwardly and put her hand on his arm. "David," she whispered, "I'm worried about you."

David couldn't keep from rolling his eyes. Jutting out his bottom jaw, he tried to decide how to handle her without exploding.

Turning to face her head-on, David shrugged and smirked, "Worried about what? Everything's fine. I'll be back to my old self as soon as I manage to get that bill paid off at the feed store."

Ida cocked her head to one side, her eyes filling with sympathy as she obviously tried to be understanding. Reaching up, she put her hands on David's shoulders and said, "It will be okay."

Putting her arms around him, Ida leaned her head against his chest and whispered, "It just seems that you've been troubled...ever since your *mamm* died."

David felt himself bristle. He definitely did not want to talk about or even think of his mother. But saying that would surely bring only more tension between them. Instead, David kept silent and let his wife hug him.

"Come on inside," Ida suggested, "Lucas is down for his nap, but he might wake up."

"I'll be in soon," David promised, trying to sound pleasant as he swallowed hard against the bitterness in his throat, "I just have to finish putting away these things."

Ida nodded and released him from her hug. Standing on tip-toe, she gave him a kiss on the cheek, "I'll go get you a sandwich ready."

David turned back to his work, anxious to have his wife back in the house.

"What is that?"

Ida's question made David's blood instantly go cold. During the split second he had looked away, she had managed to spot his bottle of whisky. David made a mad dash for the shelf, anxious to do anything to hide it, but he was too late; his wife already knew the truth.

"*Ach*, David!" She exclaimed, her face suddenly growing solemn, "I thought you'd quit."

"Drinking isn't illegal." David retorted, his internal temperature suddenly starting to rise, "I'm not a little boy, you know. You're not my parent."

"David..." Ida took a deep breath, trying to collect her thoughts, "I'm not trying to act like that. I just asked a simple question!"

"A simple question that is none of your business!"

"None of my business?" Ida returned, her eyes suddenly filling with a fire of her own, "Anything you do is my business – I'm your wife."

"Then maybe I wish you weren't!"

As soon as the words escaped David's lips, he regretted them. Turning, he grabbed a pitchfork and started mercilessly tossing hay in every direction.

"Don't you turn your back on me!" Ida exclaimed, dogging his every step, "What is that supposed to mean, David? Are you so unhappy with me as a wife that you've had to drown yourself in this?" Grabbing for the bottle of whisky, she held it up in his face, "Do you have to hide whisky out here in this barn so you'll have something to turn to when you're sick of dealing with me?"

David couldn't take it any longer. Grabbing the bottle out of her hands, he flipped it upside down, pouring all the contents on the barn floor. Tossing the empty glass bottle aside, he reached out and grabbed his wife by the arm, shaking her as he asked, "There! There you go! Are you happy now? You just made me pour it out and waste it all. There you go!"

"David," Ida's eyes were starting to fill with tears, "Let go of me, David! You're hurting me!"

Every time she tried to flinch, David tightened his grip. Gritting his teeth together, David yelled, "Are you happy with me now?" Letting his emotions get the best of him, David lifted his hand above her face.

"David!" A voice yelled out. But this time it wasn't Ida.

Looking up in surprise, David was met with the bishop and church elders standing only a few feet away watching the entire scene unfold before them.

Chapter Three

As soon as David saw the church leaders, he released his grip on his wife. He looked down at the tops of his black boots, unable to meet their stares over the weight of his shame.

"Ida," the bishop took a deep breath, obviously struggling to compose himself, "Are you all right?"

Reaching up to wipe at tears, David could hear the tremble in her voice when she whispered, "*Jah*, I'm fine. I need to get in the house to check on Lucas."

Pushing past the crowd of Amish men, Ida hurried away.

Of course, she'd leave. She wouldn't leave when David wanted her to but, as soon as she was faced with something unpleasant, she was quick to turn and make her escape. Even in his humiliation, David had to let out a snort when he thought about the irony of it all.

"David," Bishop Pete let out a deep sigh, "We need to talk. Let's make our way to the house and visit with Ida for a few minutes."

Going to the house was the last thing that David wanted to do, but he knew he would have to submit to the church leaders if he didn't want to face the *bann*. When they reached the house, Ida assured them that Lucas was still sound asleep in his bed.

Bishop Pete motioned toward the empty kitchen table, "Why don't you have a seat?"

Ida stood in the shadows, wiping her eyes and trying to gather her composure.

"Would anyone like some tea and pie?" Ida managed to ask, her voice still shaky.

Bishop Pete shook his head, "No, Ida. We're all fine. We don't just want to talk to David – we want to talk to you, as well."

David felt himself flinch as his wife pulled a chair out beside him. If she hadn't pestered him so much, the church elders wouldn't have seen such a hideous outburst! David didn't want her near him.

Bishop Pete was silent for a few moments before asking, "Ida, are you all right? Do you need anything?"

"Do you need a doctor?" One of the more outspoken elders pressured.

Ida shook her head quickly, "*Ach*, no! Goodness, I'm not hurt...just shook up is all."

Bishop Pete was the next one to ask, "Does this happen regularly, Ida?"

Ida was silent before asking, "Does what happen?"

"Does your husband beat you?" Someone else asked boldly.

David felt like crawling under the table and hiding. It would be just like Ida to lie and say that he did. She was always out to make him seem like a bad husband.

"No," Ida announced firmly, "Not at all. David has had a lot of stress...and he's seemed different since his mom died. We've always argued over the drinking, but never like this. Today was the worst things have ever been."

"How much does he drink?"

Ida shrugged, "I do not know."

"David," Bishop Pete leaned forward and studied David across the table, "how much are you drinking?"

David leaned back in his seat and let out a deep breath, "Maybe once a week," he shrugged, "Drinking is not against our Ordnung, Pete."

"I know the Ordnung better than anyone," Pete returned, "David, we came out here because some of the elders mentioned you were harsh with Ida this morning. I wanted to talk about it and see if we could help."

David grimaced inwardly when he remembered grabbing Ida's hand after the church service that morning.

"After what I just witnessed in the barn, I think it's safe to say that we truly have a bad situation developing here."

David fought the urge to jut out his bottom jaw in defiance as he tried to find the courage to stare the community leader in the eyes.

"It's got to stop, David," Pete announced firmly, pounding his fist against the table, "Before this turns into something nasty, it has to end. From here on out, you are not to react to your wife in anger. I don't know what is going on with you, but you need to work it out between yourself, God, and Ida. You are not to put a hand on Ida or Lucas unless it is done in love." Letting out a deep breath, Bishop Pete added, "And, regardless of how little you are drinking, it's obvious it's causing problems with your family. From now on, you are to buy no more alcohol and you are to drink no more alcohol."

David slowly nodded his head. What else was he supposed to do?

The bishop went on to explain that if David refused to go along with their agreement, he would face serious consequences for his behavior.

When the church leaders left, David refused to eat and went back out to the barn where he could be alone.

David had to brace himself for courage to crawl into bed that night. After an afternoon spent avoiding his wife, hiding from Ida seemed impossible when they shared the same room. His only hope was to go to sleep quickly and get the day over with.

Ida was sitting up against the hand-carved wooden headboard, her Bible propped open in her lap. Just the sight of her reading sent a wave of nausea through David. Of course, she would have to sit there, looking so arrogant as she read the Lord's book.

"Morning comes early," David muttered as he pulled the covers over himself, "Better not read for too long."

Setting her Bible aside and blowing out the lamp, Ida took a deep breath before announcing, "Well, today didn't go as well as I had hoped."

David raised his eyebrows. As far as he could see, the day had gone exactly as she had hoped. She had managed to make him look like the worst man on earth, so David was certain that her mission was accomplished.

"You know, I'm not happy about this either," Ida went on. When David didn't say anything else, Ida whispered, "I'm sorry, David. Won't you say something?"

"I don't know what to say," David announced between clenched teeth, "I'm too afraid that I might say something that would hurt you. I don't want another surprise visit from the church leaders."

After that, Ida didn't try to say anything else.

Lying in the darkness, David listened to his wife sniffle until exhaustion won out and she finally went to sleep.

Ida. Such a fine, upstanding woman in their community...and with such a passionate hared of any kind of drinks stronger than soda or homemade juice. Little Miss Perfect had never even touched the stuff. At first, David hadn't minded but, as time went by, her avoidance of alcohol seemed more and more condescending. How dare she bring up his drinking now? It was all her fault that the elders even knew he drank. That was probably her plan. She had always hated alcohol and, by pointing David's drinking out to the bishop, she was guaranteed to get her way.

Well, she might think that she knew how to keep David from drinking, but she was in for a surprise. David wasn't going to let anyone or anything keep him from doing what he wanted.

Chapter Four

Now that Ida knew where David hid his whisky, he realized that he would have to find a different hiding spot. Since he had poured out the last of it, David had his work driver pick some up for him. After getting home from work, David took it down to the cellar where he hid it in an empty cardboard box behind a row of canned fruit. David was certain it was hidden for a while.

Although things continued to stay tense between David and Ida, he felt like he could survive as long as he was still able to do what he wanted.

"*Daed*, look at this," Lucas exclaimed one night as he sat on the floor, surrounded by an assortment of farm animals, "I've got my cows all lined up."

David was sitting at the table with a pile of bills spread out in front of him.

"I think I just need a barn…" Lucas continued slowly, "Or my cows might get wet in the rain."

Ida, who was clearing away the supper dishes, motioned toward a pile of boxes by the back door, "You can use one of those. I think some of them are empty."

David was instantly alert. Suddenly looking up, he noticed Lucas grabbing for a small cardboard box. Wasn't that the box he had used to hide his alcohol? Surely not! But, when Lucas pulled it closer to his farm animals, David recognized the symbol on the side. It was the same box.

Jumping to his feet, David practically bounded across the room.

"Leave that alone!" David snapped. Reaching out, he grabbed Lucas by the arm and jerked him to his feet, pulling him away from the box and what was hidden inside.

"Where did you get that box?" David exclaimed, lifting Lucas up so he could stare him in the eyes.

Setting him down on the floor, David reached for the box and picked it up. It was empty.

"I got that box in town today!" Ida almost shouted as she ran to Lucas' side, "It's for my material."

David realized what he had done. It wasn't even the same box. The entire episode was unnecessary. Suddenly, he realized that Lucas was crying, his wails echoing throughout the house.

"David!" Ida exclaimed as she gathered the sobbing child in her arms, "*Ach*, David! What on earth is wrong with you? It is a box!"

Setting Lucas aside, Ida crossed the distance to her husband, "What are you doing? David, have you lost your mind? You nearly scared Lucas to death!"

"I didn't know!" David stormed back, unable to keep his mouth shut any longer.

"Did know what?" Ida returned, "Didn't know that it was okay for your child to play with a cardboard box?"

David found himself shaking with anger, suddenly overwhelmed by a desire to slap the arrogance right out of his wife.

Throwing her hands up in the air, Ida announced, "Lucas, let's go get you ready for bed." Although the little boy was still crying, his wailing had subsided and given way to silent sobs.

As soon as they were gone to Lucas' room, David sat down at the table and tried to turn his attention back to the stack of bills.

He couldn't believe that he had lashed out at his son like that. David could never remember a time when he had acted against his son in such a violent way.

If only Ida didn't consider drinking such a big deal, he never would have done that. It was all Ida's fault.

When David arrived home from work the next afternoon, he was surprised to find a car sitting in from of his house. The driver was out and helping Lucas put things in the trunk of her vehicle.

"What's going on?" David asked as he picked Lucas up in his arms.

"David," Ida called from the doorway of the house, "Could I talk to you for a minute?"

David set Lucas down on the ground, anxious to find a reason for the driver but also nervous about what his wife might say.

Ida was standing in the doorway, kneading her hands together nervously.

"David..." taking a deep breath, she managed to look up into his face, "David, Lucas and I are going away for a while."

David raised his eyebrows in surprise, "What do you mean?"

"We're going to stay with my parents across town for a few weeks...not for good, just long enough to work some things out..."

"You're leaving." David announced, his voice sounding completely emotionless.

"*Ach*, David, you aren't making this easy at all!" Ida announced as she reached up to cover her face with her hands, "We're not leaving...we're just taking a break."

"You're upset because I grabbed him last night?" David chuckled at how ludicrous the entire situation was, "Ida, I didn't hurt him at all. If you could have seen how hard my *daed* whipped me when I was a boy..."

Ida shook her head, "It's not like that. It's not this time I'm worried about...it's next time and the next time. David, I don't know what I'm supposed to think. Something is wrong with you and you won't even tell me what!"

"So this is all about forcing me to tell you everything I'm thinking?" David interrupted, his voice filled with bitterness.

Ida looked down at her feet, gathering her courage before she said, "You're a good dad, David. I don't want that to change. We'll be back as soon as things are different."

David threw his hands up in frustration, "Different? What does that even mean? What do you want me to do, Ida?"

"I'm firm on this one, David," Ida whispered, her voice filled with resolution, "I'm not going to let this family fall apart...and, if I have to do something extreme to keep that from happening, then I will."

David wanted to stop her. He wanted to physically grab her and hold her down, but he knew that he couldn't. The church leaders were behind her. And, if David was to act on his instinct, he realized that the police might ultimately get involved.

Stepping back, he let her walk out the door and away from their home.

Chapter Five

David had never realized how lonely their big farm house could feel. Despite the fact that he wasn't constantly confronted with Ida's nagging, he couldn't shake the utter misery of entering the house alone every night.

Each afternoon after work, David would go to Ida's parents' house to visit Lucas for a few hours. Although they said nothing, it was obvious that Ida's parents were not too thrilled with him – one day, they would be ready to beg him to make things right with their daughter, while other days they would seem closer to shooting him and making her a widow.

Although Lucas often cried to go home, he seemed to be adjusting well to their new arrangement. Several of Ida's sisters lived nearby their parents, so Lucas always had a playmate in his cousins.

Ida and David hardly spoke at all. Sometimes Ida would make an attempt at conversation, but David would cut her short with his icy, one-word replies. As far as it went, he couldn't see himself stooping to beg her to come home. If she thought he was such a terrible person that he shouldn't be in the same house as their son, David didn't see any reason to speak to her at all.

Thursday afternoon, David had just returned home from work and was out mucking a stall in the barn. His bottle of whisky sat nearby, with no reason to hide it any longer. At least he had that one benefit of being alone.

"Hello there David!" The familiar voice of Bishop Pete made David groan inwardly. Turning on his heel, he leaned his weight against the handle of the pitchfork.

"Hello Pete," he returned in a cool reception, "What can I do for you?"

"I'd like to spare a few minutes of your time to talk, if you don't mind."

Giving a shrug, David tossed the pitch-fork aside, "I don't guess I have much choice, do I?" Pausing for a moment, David continued, "If you're out here to talk to me about Ida, you're wasting your time. I don't know what I can do there."

Pete pushed back his hat so that he could rub his forehead, "David, watching you and your family...this is painful to see."

"Then don't watch," David suggested.

Pete raised an eyebrow and took a deep breath, "I'm God's chosen leader of our people. It's my job to watch. David, your family is breaking in pieces. Aren't you going to do anything to fix it before it's impossible?"

David leaded his weight against a barn post, "Pete, I don't know what you want me to do. I don't know what Ida wants me to do. Everybody acts like I need to do something...but what? I get up every morning, I go to work, and I provide for my family. I don't know what more everybody expects from me."

"Only the Lord knows how to fix this mess," Pete replied, "And you'd better be spending a lot of time figuring that out with him. David, listen to me, you are losing your wife! Doesn't that concern you at all?"

"I guess I've been prepared for this for a while," David announced, the words jumping out before he could stop them.

Pete looked at him in surprise, "What's that supposed to mean?"

"I've known for a long time that she was going to go." Somehow, David's admission was a shock even to himself.

"You knew she was going to leave and you didn't try to stop her?" Pete asked incredulously, "*Ach*, David, that makes no sense! If I knew my wife was going to leave me, I'd do everything in my power to change that!"

"I can't help it if she's not happy with me," David started to list the things that Ida did wrong and point out what a nag she could be, when he was suddenly overcome by emotion. Reaching up to try to brush at his eyes before Pete saw him crying, David managed to say, "There was no way to change anything. I just had to sit back and wait for this to happen. It's been like waiting for a storm to come...you may not like it, but it's bound to come when the clouds start gathering in the sky. And with every day that passed, it felt like I was growing more anxious just to get it over with."

Pete's brows were knit together as he muttered, "I'm not sure I understand..."

"*Ach*, Pete." David threw up his hands, "The drinking wasn't bad when I first started, but things changed...they changed and I didn't even realize it. One day, I woke up to find that I couldn't stop drinking, even if I wanted. And since then, things have been just awful."

"Does Ida know this?"

David shook his head, "No, no she doesn't! And I don't mean for her to, either. She knows I drink some, but she doesn't know that it's like this."

Taking a deep breath, Pete asked, "Do you intend to just keep going on like this forever?"

David hated Pete's question but he hated his answer even more, "I don't see that I have much of a choice."

The clucking of chicken was the only sound in the silent barn as Pete thought. Finally, he announced, "David, the church isn't just here for the fun community frolics and get-togethers...ultimately, we're here for each other. If you want to get past this...we're going to help you."

David could hardly believe what he was hearing. The fact that the bishop had heard his most awful secret and was willing to help him rather than just condemn him was almost more than David could start to grasp.

Nodding his head slowly, David took a deep breath, "At this point, I think I'm up for any kind of help I can get."

His voice growing even more serious, Pete announced, "David, most important next to having the help of the Lord, you're going to need the support of your wife."

The thought of Ida instantly made David's stomach lurch. Shaking his head vigorously, David fought the suggestion, "Not that, Pete. My wife's as good as gone. Hearing this...it will only make things worse."

Reaching out to give David a pat on the back, Pete assured him, "I don't know that it can get much worse with her. At least give it a try."

Chapter Six

Standing by the front window, David felt completely nervous as he watched his wife get out of the driver's car and start toward the house. He had gone against his better judgment and followed the bishop's suggestion by calling Ida and asking her to come over. Watching her now, David wished that he could go back in time and undo it all.

"Hello, David," Ida muttered as she stepped into the house and shut the door behind her, "Why did you call me over?" She seemed nervous, which instantly set David on alert...what did she think he was going to do, anyway?

Taking a deep breath, David motioned toward the kitchen, "I want you to see something."

Following him uncomfortable, Ida let David lead her to the kitchen where he had pile of empty bottles spread out on the table.

"*Ach*, David!" Ida exclaimed, her eyes growing large, "What on earth is that?"

"This," David announced, "Is what I have drunk since you left with Lucas. I'd like to say that I only drank this much because you took away my son, but that would be a lie. I've been drinking like this for years."

Ida let out what sounded like a gasp and shook her head, "David...that's hard for me to believe..."

"I let you think I only drank a little bit," David explained, "I'd show you a bottle every once in a while so you'd think I still had it under control. I've done that since we got married...and before that, too. When I lived at home, I had my family convinced I only drank for special events...my mom was the only one who knew the truth. She kept telling me that I would end up losing everything if I didn't stop. When she died, she made me promise her on her death bed that I would stop drinking. At that point, I truly thought I could. It was only when I tried to stop that I realized how bad off I really am."

Looking at his wife, David was surprised to see that she didn't look angry or scornful or disgusted.

"After that, I realized that she was right," David admitted, "I realized that *mamm* had it right when she told me that my drinking was going destroy my life and tear my family apart."

"What are you going to do?" Ida managed to whisper.

David shrugged, "Bishop Pete said that the church is going to help me in some way." Taking a deep breath, he managed to say, "If you want to leave, I'll understand."

To his surprise, Ida moved closer to him and reached out to put her hand on top of his.

David wasn't sure how to accept the fact that his wife wasn't ready to attack him with a sharp comment or throw his mistakes up in his face. Looking into her eyes, David remembered the reasons that he had fallen in love with her so many years ago.

Suddenly, David realized that it wasn't Ida that he didn't like. All this time, he had thought he was angry with her, but it was himself that he truly disliked.

"I'm not coming home yet, David," Ida announced slowly, "I'm not going to let Lucas be in the midst of all this. But we will come home eventually. *Ach*, David," Ida slowly shook her head, her eyes filling with tears, "When we took our marriage vows, I didn't take them lightly. I believed then that God wanted us to be together for the rest of our lives. I still believe that. I know it's going to be a struggle through all of this, but I'm going to stick with you, no matter what."

For the first time since his mother's death, David realized that he wasn't all alone. With the help of the church, his wife, and God, he would get through whatever lay ahead.

MY AMISH VISIT

SHELLY MARTIN

I drove by an old torn up sign that read "Sugar Grove, Pennsylvania: Population 566." I turned down two side streets and made a left on Trout Avenue before I found a beautiful yellow cottage that sat on Danbury Lane.

There were vines growing up the cottage and there was a small swing that sat by an old oak tree. I looked over at the neighboring farms and saw cows grazing in the fields nearby.

I didn't come to this small town to find a cowboy, I came here because I wanted to feel...something.

Something for my birth mother.

I slaved many late night hours working as a waitress at a small diner making trash for tips. I went to college then got a job at a newspaper.

All I did was study and work. I don't have a boyfriend.

I am different from most women my age. I don't party, don't curse and don't sleep around. Something always off and when I learned about the background of my birth mother things started to make sense.

I do believe that there are things we inherit from our parents other than physical characteristics. I believe we got some kind of a spiritual DNA.

I found out that my birth mother came from a community that doesn't use technology but remain tight-knit and look out for another with old-fashioned values.

Which brings me back to my siutation.

I had been feeling lonely. Most of my friends have gotten married and have children. I was a lost cause, I guess. I chose the single life over changing diapers. I gained some weight and some may say I did this to keep men away. Maybe that's true.

I like men and want to be married like my friends. But somewhere along in my journey I shut off my feelings.

My boss picked up on it. He told me that I was like an onion and not in a good way. My layers are thick and under ripe.

He told me to take a vacation. Find true emotion. If I did that, my writing would improve.

So now, I am here in the Amish community of Sugar Grove.

I walked through the door of the cottage expecting pictures of Jesus wall to wall. Instead, everything was painted a sky blue and trimmed in white. The pictures on the wall were of sunflowers and honeybees.

I expected to see a television but didn't. A small dining room table separated the two rooms. At the back of the cottage was a large bedroom. The room held a king size feather bed with all white linen, a large chest of drawers holding a large mirror. In front of the mirror were empty storage containers that were to be filled with my belongings.

In the kitchen, I noticed a note hung on the fridge. The owners said that my office called and arranged for the refrigerator to be stocked with foodstuff. I called my boss and thanked him for the kind gesture.

I milled around the cottage the rest of the evening and shot off a few e-mails before I went to sleep.

The next day I headed into town to stake out the local bakery. The front of the building had a sign that read, "Amish Bakery founded in 1848 by Tobias Hochstetler."

The structure was crafted out of natural wood and the window panes had flower boxes carved into them. The word "Bakery" was crafted out of white wooden blocks and plastered on the side of the building.

I smelled treats baking indoors and that was where I wanted to be. Bread? Cakes? What was that smell?

Another whiff told me that stew was simmering in pots on the stove in the back. I found a small table the rear of the bakery. I looked around for a plug but remembered that the Amish had no power.

I took my tablet and went on battery power, writing down my observations.

I took notice that people were walking through the doors and taking seats at various tables. The female patrons were dressed in calf length dresses that were of a solid color. They wore blue, purple and green dresses. Black bonnets over a white prayer cap. The men wore white shirts and dark pants with suspenders. When they entered they removed their hats and placed them on a rack in front of the bakery entrance.

It was only a matter of time before the place was almost full. I couldn't figure it out but there was something strange. Then it hit me.

The quietness of it all.

Everyone appeared to be either being working as a team or speaking in hushed tones. The employee's smiles appeared genuine as they greeted each table. I was amazed at how different service was compared to back in the city where people were shouting and their children were climbing over the tables.

The waiter came up to my table and greeted me as he did the others. I couldn't help but notice his sea green eyes and nice smile. His hair was cut into a shaggy style and his front tooth was slightly out of line. His skin held a golden hue from signaled he must always work long hours in the sun.

"Hello, my name is Abraham," he said, clearing his throat. "I'll be taking your order this morning, are you ready to order?"

"I'll take the breakfast puff," I said, stumbling through my words. "A banana. A cup of coffee. And a sugar cookie. And an oatmeal cookie. And the brown sugar cookie."

I didn't realize what I pig I must have sounded like but he just nodded his head as he took my menu and stepped away.

I groaned in embarrassment as I began writing on the tablet again.

"Oink, oink," I wrote. "Oink, oink.Way to impress a cute Amish boy."

Losing focus, I watched as the other patrons spoke so quietly that I had to strain my ears to hear what they were saying. When their food came, they said a word of prayer and ate in total silence.

Abraham brought my order and asked, "Is there anything else I can do for you?"

"No, thank you."

I glanced back and watched him walk away. I found that the service staff never left the front of the business. They stood at a podium and waited for tables that needed to be serviced. If a patron looked up the waiter was immediately there. No food was sent back and as the patrons left they all thanked the chef in German. I learned "denki" meant thank you and was pronounced "den-gee." Every single table wished to speak with the baker. At first, it struck me as an odd gesture but soon I realized the admiration these people had for this family.

Days turned into weeks and I continued returning to the bakery every day. I became fast friends with Hannah one of the waitresses on staff. I learned that six-year-old Mary helped prepare meals when she was not in school. I speak with Abraham when he came by my table. He often gave me his million dollar smile and a quick wave before he went into the kitchen. Sometimes he stopped and chatted with me for a moment, so today when he did I wasn't nervous or scared.

"Hello Annabelle, Have you written any new articles lately?"

"I've written a couple here and there but nothing concrete. Thank you for asking."

"I was wondering if you had any plans tomorrow. I'd like to take you on a picnic."

I noticed his cheeks turn red. Wow.

I sat there frozen in my chair for a moment. I cleared my throat before speaking.

"I'd love too," I responded shyly.

Wildflower

I didn't know what to expect from Abraham. I had never been on a date with an Amish young man before. I put the finishing touches on my make-up when I heard a horse trotting coming from down the road. I didn't want to seem eager so I left the screen door closed and sat on the couch to read a book. I opened the blinds up so I could see as he got closer. I felt the butterflies begin to swarm in my stomach as I watched the set of American Standardbred horses climb the final hill. I saw a green wagon trailing behind two horses. It was an open two-seater wagon, and even I knew that was more for romantic social calls.

The butterflies turned up a notch.

I stood and fixed a few strands of hair and checked my breath. I hadn't been on many dates in my life but I had a feeling this one was going to be life altering.

Abraham helped me into his wagon.

The seat was hard and moved when I moved. The swaying of the moving buggy caused me to grip the side. Eventually, I got used to the motion and my heart stilled. The brisk northern breeze cooled my flushed face as I took in the sights.

"Hey Abraham, how long does it take to make the bales of straw?"

"It takes one man many hours hacking the tall grass with a scythe," he said smiling. "But other farmers often pitch in and help one another. Some help even when they're unable to because they are gracious and kind individuals."

Abraham called those individuals God's disciples. I stared at this man in awe. I loved hearing him praise his community like he did because whether he knew it or not he was one of those disciples. His story reminded me of the weeks I sat at the bakery and watched the Hochstetlers as they prepared each dish with joy and hard work. I realized then that the Hochstetlers were also disciples of God. I took a deep breath in enjoying the smell of freshly cut straw mixed with Abraham's scent. He seemed to notice my hearty attempt at enjoying the scent of the countryside.

"The fresh air is nice, right?" Abraham drew in a deep breath.

"Have you worked at the dairy farm you were telling me about?" I asked curiously.

"No I haven't, I will start back again tomorrow so I won't see you again until the weekend. I only work in the bakery when work isn't available elsewhere."

A few moments later we pulled into a meadow filled with Eastern Daisies, Bearded Beggar sticks, swamp lilies, Bulbous Buttercups and Black-Eye Susans. It was full of colors. I saw reds and greens with bursts of yellow and blues. In the center of the white Elderberry and Meadow Rue sat a colorful quilt with a hand woven picnic basket on top. I looked around and saw grasshoppers jumping around and blue and yellow butterflies danced through the sky. Blue birds sat on branches twittering about.

"Oh Abraham, this is all so beautiful."

"I'm glad you like it. I wanted to find a place where I could get to know you."

I laced our hands together and we walked towards the quilt. I brushed my hands along the flowers. I stopped to smell a few; I fell down when a lady bug tickled my nose. I stayed there in that spot and looked up at the sky. What was I doing? I was busy falling in love and I forgot about my mission to find Ruth Hershberger. For now, I was going to enjoy this but I needed to use the weekdays to find out how to get in touch with Ruth.

I stood up and I continued to look around. I took everything in because I wanted to remember this day for the rest of my life. I saw his green buggy on the hillside, the cedar, and the pine trees swaying in the distance. I saw butterflies and dragonflies dancing through the sky. I watched the grasshoppers jump from flower the flower. A laugh escaped my mouth as I twirled around like a child. I felt like I had the world at the tip of my fingers.

And then there was Abraham.

He talked. I talked. He listened, paying full attention when I spoke. He never strayed from our conversations and he never looked bored.

The way he looked at me made me feel speial in a way I had never felt before.

I walked over to the quilt and sat beside Abraham. Together we talked about our hopes and dreams.

"Are you happy where you are in life?" I asked him. "Because I feel really lost."

"I was lost for some time but I prayed that one day I would figure out what I wanted and I found it. I want to open my own furniture store. Why do you feel lost?"

I got emotional. I don't know why. I felt the moisture build in my eyes for the first time since...I don't know when.

"I came to Sugar Grove in search of a woman. I'm trying to locate an Amish woman named Ruth Hershberger. I have some urgent information I need to discuss with her. She may be the woman who gave birth to me."

Abraham pulled me into his arms and I melted into his warm embrace.

"I promise that I'll help you in any way that I can," he whispered.

Abraham and I watched the sunset together. Our fingers danced together on the quilt. There were moments of silence but they were filled with laughter. Abraham always knew when my mind began wandering. He always attempted to pull me back and I was thankful for the distraction. I saw the stars form in the sky and knew our night was drawing to an end.

"Do you write books, *liebchen*?" Abraham asked.

"I haven't thought writing books lately but it was a dream of mine growing up. What does *liebchen* mean?"

"Sorry," he blushed I couldn't help it."

"What does it mean?"

"It means 'my love.'"

"Liebchen sounds better than my love if you ask me."

I learned he wanted to work with animals and wished one day to be a veterinarian. The money wasn't there so he wasn't sure how he could pull it off.

He looked at the sky and announced it was time to start heading home. The buggy ride home was silent but in a good way. I could see fireflies lighting up the sky and could hear crickets chirping in the night. This night felt too good to be true. It felt absolutely bewitching. When they made it to her cottage we heard an owl hooting nearby.

"I never heard such a noise in person," I laughed. I was used to horns honking, sirens blaring, and the usual city noises. I started to enjoy looking up and seeing the constellations in the sky and hearing the animals and insects talk in the night. It felt like a whole other universe out here. A universe I either never noticed or forgot about.

Abraham pulled up to the little yellow cottage on Danbury Lane and walked me to the door. He looked a little nervous before he finally spoke up.

"Would you like to attend Sunday Worship with my family? It is always nice to listen to the bishop tell tales about *Herr Gott*."

"Yes, I would love to join your family on Sunday."

"Perhaps you will see Ruth there."

"Perhaps I will."

Kiss Me

The week was long and brutal. I continued going to the bakery even though I knew Abraham wouldn't be there. I was glad Abraham wasn't here because could focus on finding Ruth. I looked through the local phone book and found a Hershberger family that lived in Sugar Grove. Their address was close by but I could feel myself cowering down. I also didn't want to march up to Ruth and say "Hi, I'm your daughter."

I learned enough to know that the Amish were close knit and they weren't keen on outsiders meddling in their business.

I woke up early Sunday morning and took a bubble bath. I was daydreaming about spending the day with the Hochstetlers and learning about the Amish community

I heard a knock on the door and put on my robe before I heard my name being called.

"Annabelle, are you in there?" said a deep male voice.

I recognized that voice but I wasn't dressed to meet him at the door. I stood behind the closed door and answered back.

"Abraham is that you?"

The last time I looked at the clock it had been six a.m. Who would be here so early?

"Yes, it is Abraham are you alright?" He sounded scared.

"I just got out of the shower, I'm going to unlock the doors and go back to my room. Count to sixty and then you can come in."

Abraham busted out laughing and then I heard his faint counting. I ran to the back of the cottage and slammed the door closed. I grabbed my dress off of the hanger and threw it over top of me. I started pulling curlers from my hair when I heard water running in the kitchen. I was curious about that but opted to put on my shoes and fix my hair instead.

Abraham helped me into the buggy. We trotted the three miles to his family farm and picked up his sisters Hannah and Mary. The girls looked a little flustered but neither said a word at first. Hannah broke the silence.

"Grosseldre and Maemm rode with Daed to the Yoder bauereie."

Mary apologized when she interrupted her sister but she saw Annabelle's uncomfortable shifting.

"Hannah, our guest doesn't speak Pennsylvania Dutch perhaps you should use Englisch."

Hannah's faced reddened before she apologized.

"Our grandparents rode with our parents to the Yoder Farm so we don't need to pick them up this morning."

"Mary, that was kind of you to include Annabelle into the conversation, *Herr Gott* is smiling down on you for your acts of kindness."

The buggy pulled onto a large farm and parked next to the other rows of wagons. The farm was beautifully maintained. There are usually animals roaming about but today they were confined to the barn. Worship was held on that warm summer morning because there were two hundred people that showed up to hear the bishop speak.

After he finished, children began playing a game in a nearby field. Men helped with farm work as the women prepared the covered dishes.

I took a tour of the farm then walked back to the others. Then I saw a woman who looked vaguely familiar. She was helping a small child fix his clothes near the outhouse. I waited until the child ran off before trying to speak with the woman. Maybe she knew Ruth or perhaps she is Ruth. There was something that was pulling me in the direction of that woman. I was about to greet her but she took one look at me, turned and walked away.

I felt as if I were punched in the stomach.

I felt couldn't breathe, I looked for the only one who knew my secret.

"Abraham, I am so sorry, but do you think you could take me home? I'm not feeling well."

"I need to let my parents know but I'll meet you at the buggy."

The next day, Abraham stopped by and asked if I wanted to take a walk.

He led me down a dirt road before we hit a walking trail. Then he took my hand before speaking.

We walked and talked for a while before Abraham spotted a stream. He found a large leaf and made a bowl out of it so that we could enjoy the water. We were walking again this time he took her with confidence and kissed it. We walked for a long time before I asked,

"Are we walking to my home in LA?"

"Come we will rest before we head back to your house," Abraham laughed.

He was used to long hours of walking but he understood that she wasn't accustomed to it.

"What happened today at the Yoder farm?"

"I tried to speak to this woman who looked familiar, but she ran away."

He said nothing, leading me to a hay field were we sat and rested.

I pulled a piece of straw lose and gathered the courage to see where this relationship was going.

"Have you ever been in love?" I asked timidly.

Abraham smiled like he was just pondering the topic himself.

"Yes, I have been in love," he smiled. "This woman brightens the sky when she steps into the sunlight. She lights up a room when she walks in with a smile on her face. I hear her heart beats and my world feels absolute. She walks barefoot in the sand and has skin the color of ivory. Her eyes are the color of storm clouds on a hot summer's day. Her lips look like ripe cherries ready for tasting."

He leaned over and caressed my cheek.

I didn't know what to say.

"Annabelle Michaels, I love you more than I ever thought possible. I'd rather die a lonely man before I'd ever give you up."

"I don't know what to say."

"We had better start back before it gets too late," he said. "I have to work in the morning and you need to find Ruth."

Deception

The next morning I woke up feeling fresh and determined. I decided to take matters into my own hands. I decided to go to the Hershberger farm and meet this family. I pulled out a cookbook from the cabinet. I decided to make a chicken casserole to show respect for their family. It took me a few hours to get things together and it was almost lunch time. I loaded the rental car and drove to the address I found the other day.

I pulled up to the farm and knocked on the door. The paint was peeling from the wood and the hinges were rusted. There was a large run-down barn behind the house and there was a fenced off area on one side of the house. I knocked again and shouted a greeting. An elderly woman came to the door; she spoke little English and told me to go around back.

I walked over to the fenced area.

"Hello, is anyone here?"

I heard the woman talking to a man in hushed tones but the man turned and walked away, but not before I could see tension rise in his shoulders.

I took a deep breath and she walked up to the woman I saw the other day.

"Good afternoon, I am Annabelle Michaels and I work with the LA Times. I'd like to write a story on your dairy farm if that is ok with you. We want to determine if there is a large difference in the way milk is produced."

The woman chuckled before responding

"I know you came here because you want to know if you're my boppli. I know you want to know if I am your Maemm."

Before I could answer I saw someone coming toward me out of the corner of my eye.

Abraham.

I couldn't believe it Abraham knew Ruth all along. I had to know why he didn't tell me but right now I just wanted him to know that I now know his secret.

I walked over to him and asked to speak with him alone. He said he needed to finish his shift and he would come to the cottage so we could talk.

I drove the three miles back to the cottage in tears, I had learned who Ruth was, and I learned Abraham was manipulative and he kept things from those he loved. Neither obviously loved me or cared for me or they would have been honest from the start.

I curled up on the couch waiting to hear from the airlines. I was booking a ticket and getting out of this small town.

Then I heard a feint knock at the door. I opened the door and there standing was not Abraham but Ruth; my birth mother was standing right in her doorway. It was the one thing I always wanted and often dreamed of. I didn't care if I had the perfect man or the comfiest shoes. I just wanted to be accepted by the woman who gave up on me.

I invited Ruth in and listened to her tale that began twenty-three years ago. I learned my dad was a fisherman and my parents met when my dad delivered fish to the local market. He would often purchase jam from her mom's fruit stand and one time he bought all her jam. He stopped by each summer for three years before her mom finally grew the courage to leave her roots and locate the man that filled her soul. My mother found my father and she claimed he was the love of her life but she only had a few short months with him. She felt punished by God when they discovered he had colon cancer. Her mom had just discovered she was pregnant with me when her father told her the news. My father stayed with my mom for the first two months but when he died my mother was forced to live in a women's shelter until she gave birth. She put me up for adoption and when I was adopted Ruth moved back to her parents and joined the Amish community.

Ruth admitted that she never mentioned me until Abraham confronted her a few weeks ago. Ruth learned I was getting impatient and wanted to meet her but Ruth was ashamed that she hid her secret for so long. That was when Ruth told her story to the community and to her husband. He knew of her relationship with my father but he was unaware she conceived a child. I drew in a deep breath and immediately thought of Abraham.

There was a knock on the door and we both knew who it was. I opened the door and ushered him to the swing that faced the hills.

"Abraham, how long have you known about her being my mom?"

His shoulders sank then he fell to his knees. I saw tears escape his eyes, but there was no way I was going to let him get away that easily. No matter how much I loved this man, he kept something from important from the person he swore he loved.

"*Liebchen*, I realized the day that you mentioned your birth mother's name. I won't lie, I knew who she was, but I wanted to make sure it was the right person. I didn't want to accuse someone of something she never did. Once I discovered she was the woman you were searching for I asked her to come to you when she was ready because it's her news to share. I wasn't around then and I don't know much now. I do know that there is much she eager to tell and in time I'm sure she will. We both care deeply about you and are worried you will leave. I'm sorry I kept any information from you, I only did it out of protection."

I looked into his eyes as he faced me and I saw the same passion as when he told me about God's disciples. He was helping a friend in need. This friend just happened to be my mother.

I hadn't seen real feeling until I saw this man's face. It was full of emotions, guilt mixed with grief and a face stained with tears. He held onto my leg like it was the only thing holding us together. I could turn cold and run away but instead, I dropped to my knees and placed my head on his chest. All I wanted was Abraham and Ruth in my life. I looked up and I kissed him hard. I fell into his arms and confessed.

"Abraham Thomas Hochstetler, *Ich liebe dich,* than one could love one's self."

I used the Dutch phrase for I love you trying to prove my devotion to his heritage.

"I think of you daily and I pray for your safety each night. I hold you in my heart where I've held no other. There is no way I would turn and walk away. I want to be a part of your life."

He got down on one knee and took my hand in his.

"Annabelle Naomi Michaels Hershberger, will you marry me?"

CALL OF THE AMISH

ELIZA FITZGERALD

Part One:

The call came in the middle of the night. Somehow Elizabeth King's daed had heard the telephone ringing in his shop, and had hurried from bed to answer it. He had the only phone for miles around, and often when the phone rang there was an emergency that needed tending to, though just as often someone from the community hurried to their house to use the phone as well.

"Elizabeth, wake up, my girl."

Elizabeth squinted into the sudden brightness, and for a moment she was so disoriented that she had no idea where she was or who was talking to her. Then she realized that her maemm was kneeling beside her bed with a kerosene lantern shining.

"What is it, Maemm?" Elizabeth asked.

"Your cousin, Melissa, she needs your help," her maemm replied. "Her babe is coming early, and there isn't enough time to get her to the birthing center that she chose in the city. She's refusing to go to the local hospital, and you're the only midwife she knows. Hurry now, and get dressed, girl. Your daed is getting the buggy ready to take you."

Elizabeth felt her eyes go wide and round as she drew in a sharp breath. Thoughts whirred through her mind as she slipped from beneath the covers of her bed, careful not to jostle her sister, Sarah, who grumbled in her sleep and turned toward the wall. As Elizabeth slipped into her dress and tucked her hair up into her kapp, she looked at her maemm.

"I don't know if I'm ready for this, Maemm," she whispered, feeling her stomach form into a tight knot.

"The Lord has delivered you to this point," her maemm said. "Pray that He will guide your work, and remember that all you do is in the glory of His name."

Elizabeth nodded, kissed her maemm on the cheek, and hurried down the stairs to get her shawl from where it hung on a peg by the front door. Her daed was already in the driver seat of the buggy, waiting in the moonlight to drive her quickly into town where her Englischer cousin was waiting for her.

As her daed drove along shadowy lanes, Elizabeth bowed her head, and silently prayed, "*Dear Lord, I am scared. I have never done this by myself before, and I need You to be with me. I need You to guide my hands. Please lift up Melissa and her unborn babe. Let me be an instrument of Your peace. Let me do this well, Lord. Please, oh, please. Amen.*"

When she got done with her prayer, she clenched her fists together on her lap, pulling her shawl tighter around her shoulders. Elizabeth had never been so terrified of anything in her whole life, but at the same time she felt a sense of peace descend upon her. In that moment, she knew, she just knew that the Lord had heard her prayer. He had created her for this moment.

Her daed pulled the buggy up in front of Melissa's house, the electric laws all blazing, and Melissa's husband, Jim, on the front porch, pacing. When he caught sight of her, he jogged down the stairs, and put his arm around her. "Elizabeth! I'm so glad that you are here," Jim said. "She's saying that she's going to have the baby any moment."

"Did you get the items together that were on the birthing center's list?" Elizabeth asked, calmly.

Jim nodded, his head bobbing up and down. He looked so helpless that Elizabeth felt sorry for him. She shrugged out of her shawl and handed it to him. "Good," Elizabeth said, rolling up her sleeves. "Are you going to stay in the room? I'm sure that Melissa would find that helpful."

"Anything," Jim said. "Just tell me what I need to do, and I'll do it."

Taking a deep breath, Elizabeth walked into the bedroom where Melissa was moaning softly as she lay on the bed. With a quick glance at her cousin, all of Elizabeth's cool, collected calm seemed to flee. She murmured another quick prayer.

"Hello, cousin," Elizabeth said in a soft tone as she entered the darkened room. She paused to allow her cousin to register her appearance, but also to gauge the situation that lay before her. "Melissa," she continued in a firmer voice. "You are going to be just fine. I'm going to open these curtains to let in some light." Elizabeth wasn't sure why, but it felt right to let light in. Her mind flickered to one of her favorite Bible verses [something about letting your light shine]

When Elizabeth got closer to the bed, Melissa opened her eyes and reached out to grip Elizabeth's hand. "Thank you for coming," Melissa said through gritted teeth as another contraction ripped through her small body. "Lizzy, I don't know if I can do this."

Hearing her cousin call her by her childhood nickname brought Elizabeth soundly into the present, and a sense of peace descended on her. She reached out and smoothed her cousin's sweaty curls away from her forehead. "You can do this," she said. "And you will."

Part Two:

"It was the most amazing experience I've ever had, Paul," Elizabeth said with a contented sigh as she leaned back against the seat of Paul's buggy. She could still feel the rush of adrenaline that had coursed through her veins as Melissa pushed the baby girl out into Elizabeth's hands. When she had handed the baby to her cousin, tears had run rivulets down both of their cheeks. Jim had cut the cord, and beamed with the pride of a new father, though Elizabeth had caught the relief in his eyes too. He hadn't been able to stop thanking her.

"I just know that this is what God brought me into the world to do," she added. Then she turned to her beau, the boy she had grown up with, fallen in love with, and expected to marry as soon as he took over his daed's farm. She expected to see her own excitement reflected in his eyes; he had always been her biggest cheerleader, especially as she had embarked on her journey to become a midwife.

Instead, Paul gazed at her with serious eyes and his mouth drawn into a tight frown. "Elizabeth," he said, drawing out the syllables of her name as he often did when he thought she was being silly.

"What?" she asked, her eyebrows furrowing. She thought that Paul would have been excited for her. She thought he would have seen the importance of the event through her eyes. She had thought they had the same vision for their future. It seemed to her now that she thought wrong.

"God brought you into the world to be my wife," Paul said softly.

Elizabeth's confusion amplified. There was a buzzing in her ears that she didn't like. "God created me to be many things," she said, her breath feeling hollow in her chest.

"Of course," Paul said in a cajoling tone, but something in his expression made her think that he didn't believe that.

"You know that I can't wait to be your wife," Elizabeth said. "But the feeling I got delivering Melissa's baby, well, I can't even describe it. There are no words for being a witness to a miracle like that. Doing that over and over would be an amazing way to live."

Paul turned toward her in the carriage seat. He reached out to take her hands in his own. "Elizabeth, it's fine for you to do midwife work right now, but what happens after we get married? You'll have a household to run. And what happens when we begin to have children?"

The starkness of his words made Elizabeth pause. She knew that he had a point, and she wasn't going to disagree with him on that point. But she wasn't willing to concede that she should give up being a midwife just because her life would be busier.

Slowly she said, "I can't wait to have a home and children of our own, but I just can't see how being a midwife wouldn't be able to fit into that picture."

Paul pressed his lips together. "You'll simply be too busy." He said it in a tone that made it clear that he thought that was all there was to say on the matter, but that fact made Elizabeth even more upset.

"God doesn't just create us for one purpose," Elizabeth said. "I'm sorry, Paul, but I just don't think that I agree with you."

The look on Paul's face went from disapproving to impassive. Elizabeth had never seen him act like this before, and she didn't like it one bit. "I think you should take me home now," she said, drawing her hand away. Turning her face away from him, she pressed her lips together. If she said something now, she knew that there was a chance that she would say something that she would regret.

Paul didn't move for a long moment. So long, in fact that Elizabeth almost looked over at him, but instead she held firm. Finally he heaved a sigh, and flicked the reins. As the buggy moved off down the road, Elizabeth felt a rush of tears flood her eyes. Blinking rapidly so they wouldn't fall, she tried to figure out a way to make Paul understand where she was coming from, but her mind was a blank.

Instead she decided to pray. "*Dear Lord, I don't understand what is happening right now. Paul has always been my soul mate, the one that I know I'm destined to be with. And yet, today I know that You showed me another part of Your plan for me. How do I make Paul see this? How do I explain it? The feeling that delivering Melissa's baby gave me? Where are you leading me, Lord? Please show me the way. Amen.*"

When she finished praying, Elizabeth felt a sense of peace descend on her. She drew a deep breath, and said, "Paul, I don't know how to explain this feeling to you, but I know that what I did today came from God. I don't want things to be bad between us, but right now this is the path that He is leading me down. I...I think that we should spend a bit of time apart."

"How can you say that?" Paul asked with a gruffness in his voice that Elizabeth knew well. He did that when he was trying to keep the hurt at bay. She had never caused him pain before, and the realization made her heart ache. Yet she wasn't going to back off.

"I just know in my heart that if we're going to have a future together then we need to trust in the Lord and His plan for us," Elizabeth said.

Just as she finished speaking, the buggy turned into the drive for Elizabeth's house. When Paul reined the horse in, Elizabeth was quick to get out on her own. She hurried into the house without looking back. She needed to keep her resolve, and she knew that if she looked back, her heart might break.

Part Three:

"Gross-mammi? Can I talk to you?" Elizabeth leaned on the kitchen door jamb of her grandmother's house.

"Of course, dear," her gross-mammi said, glancing over her shoulder at her. She continued to mix the butter into the flour for the pie crust that she was making.

Elizabeth grabbed an apron off a hook on the wall as she entered the kitchen, and tied it around her waist. One of the rules about entering Gross-mammi's kitchen was that one had to help when they came in. No matter what. No matter who. Elizabeth had never minded. She found the act of baking with her grandmother soothing.

Reaching for a paring knife, Elizabeth began to slice strawberries for the berry pie her grandmother was preparing. "I delivered my cousin Melissa's baby yesterday," she said.

"Your daed told me," Gross-mammi said with a nod. "I'm proud of you, my girl. That's God's work."

Elizabeth felt a burst of joy in her chest. "I felt like God was touching my hands," she said, tears welling at the memory. "I can't think of a better way to describe it."

She finished cutting the strawberries, added them to the bowl with the blueberries and raspberries, and poured in a cup of sugar. As she was coating the berries her grandmother reached across the counter, and tapped her hand. Elizabeth glanced up at her beloved gross-mammi, and she could see the question in the older woman's eyes.

With a sigh, Elizabeth wiped her hands on her apron, and said, "I'm having a problem with Paul." As soon as she said the words, tears flooded her eyes. Unable to keep them in, they ran rivulets down her cheeks. Swiping at them with the heels of her hands, Elizabeth slumped over the counter, leaning her elbows on the floury surface.

"Oh, is that all?" Gross-mammi asked, waving her hand in the air. Elizabeth looked at her grandmother with surprise. The older woman continued, "A little lovers' spat, no?"

Elizabeth swiped at her leaky eyes again. "I don't know," she said unable to keep the misery out of her voice. "He doesn't like the idea of my being a midwife. At least not after we get married. If we get married, I guess. I just couldn't get him to understand how much I feel like God has called me to deliver babies, to be His hands in the world. Am I wrong, Gross-mammi?"

Her grandmother was silent, silent and still for a long time before she picked up the bowl of berries and poured them into the pie crust. Finally she said, "I think that only the Lord can answer that question, my dear. My advice to you is to pray. Pray hard, and then listen. Listen with all your heart and soul. If you do that, then I'm sure that you will find the answer that you seek."

Watching her grandmother put the pie into the oven, Elizabeth felt peace descend upon her. She knew that her gross-mammi's advice was sound and true. She did need to pray. And yet...right now she also needed her grandmother's comforting presence. And she needed pie.

"Is there any cleaning you need done, Gross-mammi?" Elizabeth asked. If she could distract herself by helping her grandmother, then she could perhaps calm her racing mind down enough to let her soul catch up. Then she could pray.

"Would you mind bringing down the rugs, and giving them a good beating?" Elizabeth was sure that she could see a smile hovering around her gross-mammi's mouth. The rugs probably didn't need to be beaten, but Elizabeth was glad for the opportunity to work out some of her frustration.

"Of course," Elizabeth said as she headed into the front room to get the first rug. Rolling it up, she hefted it over her shoulder.

Over and over, Elizabeth retrieved rug after rug, hung them on the clothesline, and beat the dust and dirt out of them. By the time she was done, she was exhausted and sweaty, but she also felt calmer. After she had placed the last rug back in the upstairs guest bedroom, Elizabeth jogged back down the stairs.

"All done, Gross-mammi," she called as she came into the kitchen.

"Just in time," her grandmother said. "The pie just came out of the oven. Come, sit with me, and we'll have a slice."

"Great," Elizabeth said with a grin.

The two women sat together, and for a long stretch of time Elizabeth felt soothed, which was exactly what she had hoped to feel when she came here. But then thoughts of Paul started to creep back in. By the time she was taking her last bite of pie, she was having trouble swallowing. As if her gross-mammi could read her thoughts, she reached over and patted Elizabeth's hand again.

"Just remember to pray," Gross-mammi said. "The Lord will give you all the answers that you need. Just a moment." Elizabeth threaded her hands together as she watched her grandmother leave the room. A moment later she returned with a large Bible in her hands.

Opening it, she said, "I think this will help you. Ecclesiastes 3: 1-8, 'To every thing there is a season, and a time to every purpose under the heaven 2 A time to be born, and a time to die; a time to plant, and a time to pluck up that which is planted;3 A time to kill, and a time to heal; a time to break down, and a time to build up;4 A time to weep, and a time to laugh; a time to mourn, and a time to dance;5 A time to cast away stones, and a time to gather stones together; a time to embrace, and a time to refrain from embracing;6 A time to get, and a time to lose; a time to keep, and a time to cast away;7 A time to rend, and a time to sew; a time to keep silence, and a time to speak;8 A time to love, and a time to hate; a time of war, and a time of peace.'"

"I've always liked that one," Elizabeth agreed. As she kissed her grandmother goodbye, Elizabeth felt calm once again. She needed to pray.

Part Four:

Dear Lord, Elizabeth prayed as she walked toward her closest friend, Miriam's, house. *I know that You are the designer of my life. I want to trust in the path that You have laid out for me. I believe, Lord, help me in my unbelief. I know that I am a sinner, and that I try to assert my own will instead of listening to You. I want to change, though, Lord. I ask you to show me what path You want for me. Should I be a midwife? Or should I marry Paul? Or...Lord, I know that it is asking a lot, but is there a way that I could have both? I'm listening, Lord. Show me the way. Amen.*

Elizabeth swallowed as she finished her prayer. It wasn't that prayer was foreign to her; she prayed often and with fervent sincerity. She had meant what she had prayed, that she was a sinner who all too often tried to fit her will onto that of the Lord's. But she had also meant her plea for help. Now she had to clear her head—and heart—to listen and hear the Lord's answer.

By the time she got to Miriam's house, Elizabeth still felt as confused as ever. She couldn't help feeling like she wanted to press the Lord for an answer right now, but she knew all that would get her was a lesson in being patient.

"Elizabeth!"

Miriam clattered down the front steps, and threw her arms around Elizabeth. For a moment all of her stress melted away as she hugged her friend back. This was what she needed, desperately. Perhaps that was why she had felt such an overwhelming desire to visit Miriam today. The thought occurred to her so fast that Elizabeth almost missed it. Maybe this was the Lord answering some part of her prayer. Maybe she needed to listen to what Miriam had to say. Miriam had gone through more in her young life than most people would in all their years so Elizabeth definitely trusted her friend's perspective.

"My maemm told me that you delivered your cousin's baby," Miriam said. "How wonderful! Come sit in the garden, and I'll go get some lemonade and cookies. You'll have to tell me all about it."

Elizabeth smiled, feeling relief wash over her. "Let me help," she said.

With a firm shake of her head, Miriam said, "Go sit in the garden. You're my guest. Let me get the refreshments."

Knowing that it was futile to argue with Miriam, Elizabeth headed toward the garden as her friend went to the house. Miriam and her family lived on the edge of their small town on a large farmette. Miriam's daed owned a popular furniture shop that was busy with tourists all through the summer months.

Chickens scattered as Elizabeth crossed the stone path toward the large kitchen garden that Miriam's maemm had spent years cultivating. Elizabeth sat down at the small wicker table set under a big willow tree. A moment later Miriam joined her.

Setting the lemonade and cookies under the tree, Miriam said, "So, tell me all about it. How was it delivering a baby for the first time?"

"It was beyond anything I can even explain," Elizabeth said, feeling a rush of pleasure as she remembered the experience. "It was like...like I was actually the Hands of God. Like He was guiding all my movements. I loved every second of it. I can't wait to do it again." Her smile faded as she thought about Paul.

"What's wrong?" Miriam asked, clearly seeing her friend's sudden distress.

Elizabeth sighed. "Paul wasn't very happy with my first experience."

"Why not?" Miriam held out the plate of cookies toward Elizabeth.

"He doesn't think that I can do both midwifery and being his wife," she said.

"Did he propose?" Miriam asked around a mouthful of cookie, her eyes widening.

Shaking her head, Elizabeth said, "No. I'm sure he's going to one day. Probably sooner rather than later, but he might not since he doesn't like the idea of my being a midwife. I wish that I could make him understand that what I'm doing when I deliver babies is God's work. I don't feel like it would detract from my duties as his wife."

Miriam bit into another cookie, and tipped her head to one side as she appeared to consider the situation. Elizabeth sucked in her breath as she waited to hear what her friend thought. What if Miriam felt the same way as Paul? That would only add to her confusion. The suspense grew as the silence stretched, and Elizabeth felt a knot tighten in her stomach.

Finally Miriam said, "I'm sure that Paul feels scared."

Her words shocked Elizabeth for a moment. Then she furrowed her brow, and said, "What do you mean?"

Taking a sip of her lemonade, Miriam shrugged. "It seems pretty clear to me. God has given you an incredible gift. You've found your calling. Most people wait their entire lives to find their calling. Paul has thought of you as his calling for your whole lives. To be married to you is what he is called to do."

"I always thought that too," Elizabeth said softly. "And I still do. I just wonder...can't God call us to more than one thing."

"Of course," Miriam said, waving her hand in the air. "There is a season for everything, so why can't we have more than one calling in our lives."

"My gross-mammi said almost the exact same thing," Elizabeth said. "I just wish that I could make Paul understand that."

"Maybe it's not so much about making Paul understand, but putting the situation entirely in God's hands," Miriam said.

"What do you mean?" Elizabeth wiped the cookie crumbs off her skirt as she looked at her friend.

"Well, you just need to do your best at what God is asking of you right now," Miriam said. "Paul needs to do the same. When the Lord is ready for the two of you to be together, you will be."

"You're so smart," Elizabeth told her friend. "I knew there was a reason that I wanted, no, needed, to come here today."

Miriam grinned at her. "You know I'm always here to help you if you need it," she said.

Elizabeth squeezed her friend's hand. She did know, and more than that she knew that the Lord had given her such a friend just for situations like this. She whispered a quick prayer of thanks before she reached for another cookie.

Part Five:

"I don't understand why you won't come out with me today," Paul said.

Looking at him as he stood at the bottom of the porch steps made Elizabeth's heart ache, but she had to keep in mind the advice that Gross-mammi and Miriam had given her. She had to follow God's plan for her, and she needed to stay strong on that. If that didn't mean that Paul was a part of that right now, then she needed to accept that and be strong.

"Because there's a baby over at the Hoestetler homestead that needs to be delivered," Elizabeth explained.

Paul frowned up at her. "I thought you had decided not to do midwifery anymore."

"Jean is one of my very best friends. You know that. Of course I need to be there." Elizabeth returned Paul's frown. The ache in her heart increased and stole her breath. Why would God let her feel so much pain? Cause so much pain between the two of them? Elizabeth knew that He was a good and loving God, so why would it be that He would allow such heartache to exist in the world?

And yet, Elizabeth knew that pain existed because of the sin of Adam and Eve. She was a sinner, so why should she expect any special treatment? "Paul," she said in a soft voice, "I truly believe that this is what God is calling me to do right now. I can't say if this is what God will always ask me to do, and I do think that you and I are called to be together, but I need to answer His call."

Paul's frown deepened, but he didn't argue with her. Instead he seemed to be listening to what she had to say. Finally he asked, "So what does that mean for us right now?"

"Right now?" Elizabeth repeated. She could sense the hurt in Paul, and she thought of what Miriam had said. If he was hurting as much as she was, then she didn't want to make it worse. "I think it means that we both need to pray deeply, and listen with all our hearts to what the Lord is telling us. Then we follow His plan, His path, His will for our lives. When it's time for us to come back together, He will let us know."

Paul nodded. "Can I still come to see you every Sunday?" he asked in a cracking voice that shattered Elizabeth's voice.

"Of course," she said. "And we'll keep talking about where God is leading us."

Elizabeth tried hard to put the whole conversation with Paul out of her mind as she delivered Sarai's baby that afternoon. Her good friend Jean helped, but seemed nervous to be attending her own sister's labor. After the little boy had been placed safely in his mother's arms, Elizabeth sank into a sofa in the parlor. Jean brought her a glass of tea and a muffin.

Jean sat down on a chair nearby, and the two of them ate in contented silence. When they were done, Elizabeth said, "I definitely know that God is leading me down this path right now."

The curious look on Jean's face made Elizabeth giggle, though she suspected that she was really just very tired. Elizabeth explained, "I've been praying that God would show me my path in life. I feel called to two such paths actually. Being a midwife is what I'm supposed to do right now, but I know that one day I'll marry Paul. I think that he is finally starting to understand that we can't impose our will on God's plans for us."

"That's not something we can ever do, is it?" Jean said.

"The thing that really bothers me about the whole situation," Elizabeth said, "is that Paul is so hurt by it all, and that's truly not what I want."

"You aren't hurting him on purpose," Jean said as if this was a fact that was obvious. "Unfortunately God's plan, if you truly want to submit to His will, bypasses all other plans."

"I know," Elizabeth agreed. "But do you suppose that there is a way to lessen his pain?"

Jean considered the question. "I'm sure that you are already doing it, but I would advise you to pray. Pray hard and listen hard."

Elizabeth nodded seriously. "I have been, and I'll continue to do it."

"Do you think that God is asking you to take some part away from each other for a while?" Jean asked.

The adrenaline from the delivery was wearing off, leaving Elizabeth with a bone deep exhaustion setting in. "No, I don't think that at all," she said.

"So, can't you just keep spending time together? And when it's time for the two of you to get married, you'll just know," Jean suggested.

"I guess I hadn't really thought about that," Elizabeth said with a frown. "That seems quite stupid of me, doesn't it?"

Jean shrugged. "Sometimes the most obvious solutions evade us."

"My biggest problem is that I don't know if Paul will feel the same way," Elizabeth said. "He's been so hurt by my midwifery."

"Maybe he just needs time to get used to it," Jean said. "You've just started. How many babies have you delivered so far?"

"Just two," Elizabeth said.

"Then time will help him accept this part of your life," Jean said firmly.

Elizabeth felt better as soon as Jean spoke. "You know, Jeannie, you are so smart."

Jean grinned at her. "I know," she replied. "But thanks that's nice of you to say."

As Elizabeth sank back into the sofa and felt her eyes drift closed, she offered up a prayer of thanks to the Lord that He had given her such good friends and advisors. How did she deserve such good things?

Part Six:

Three more babies were delivered in the next three weeks, and Elizabeth felt more certain than ever that God had called her to be a midwife. Things between her and Paul had been different, but not as bad as she had feared. Though he had been visiting less often, the visits that they did have seemed better to her. If pressed, she wasn't sure she would have been able to say exactly what seemed better, though there were little signs that Paul was beginning to understand how much being a midwife meant to her.

So when Paul pulled up the driveway in a new buggy, Elizabeth felt her heart stir with excitement and delight. She came out onto the porch as he jumped down. "What do you think?" he asked with an easy grin that she hadn't seen in weeks.

"It's lovely," she said. "When did you get it?"

"Yesterday," Paul said. He was happy, his eyes crinkling in the corners. There was a giddy energy coming off of him that reminded her of a child. "Can you come for a ride? Right now?"

Elizabeth laughed. She couldn't help it. He looked so happy. "Let me just grab my shawl."

Paul helped her up into the buggy. "Isn't it roomy?" he asked when they were both settled.

Glancing at the back seat, Elizabeth nodded. "It's great. It must have cost you a fortune," she said.

"I've been saving for it for a while," Paul admitted. "Actually I was praying that God would show me the right time to buy it, and recently I felt that it was time."

"I'm glad," Elizabeth said. She felt a momentary flash of surprise and disappointment that she wasn't included in the decision making process. Then she realized that Paul was doing exactly what she had asked him to do. He was listening for God's will in his life just as she had been doing in hers. The part of her that had felt so jealous of his decision a moment before suddenly rejoiced in it.

"It's big for a good reason," Paul was saying. Elizabeth realized with a guilty start that she hadn't been paying attention as he waxed lyrical about the many wonderful features of the buggy, which she was sure was top of the line. Paul probably had a reason for every choice that he had made; that was one of the many qualities that she loved about him.

"Oh?" Elizabeth said.

He nodded, and gave her a smile even as they lapsed into silence. They drove to the top of the highest hill in the county. The two of them had been coming here since they had first started courting, and Elizabeth still felt it was the most romantic place she could ever imagine.

As Paul pulled the horse to a stop, he half turned on the bench seat so that he was mostly facing her. "My maemm told me that you delivered another baby yesterday," he said. "How is that going?"

Elizabeth couldn't keep the surprise from her face as she said, "Amazing. It's still amazing."

Paul was quiet for such a long time that Elizabeth thought that he might be trying to come up with yet another way to talk her out of continuing to pursue being a midwife. Then he ran a hand along the back of his neck. "I'm sorry," he said. "I was wrong to try to stop you from doing something that you are so obviously meant to do. The truth is, well, the truth is that I was scared. I was scared that if you found something that was more important than me that I might lose you forever."

Miriam and Jean had been spot on with their assessment of the situation. Elizabeth reached across the seat to take Paul's hand. "I'm sorry that I didn't stop to listen to you and your concerns," she said. "I mean, really listen. The way you deserved."

"That's partly my fault. I was so blinded by my fears that I pressed you for something that I had no right to ask. I should have been listening to the Lord first, and then talking to you about everything in a calm and open manner," Paul said.

"Thank you for that," Elizabeth said. "But I think that what I should have said is that I understand that change can be scary, but also that I don't think God gives us just one calling in our lives. I think that He calls us to different things throughout our lives."

"That's a faithful thought," Paul said.

"Miriam planted that seed for me. I've been praying about it for weeks, and I see that the more I pray and listen, the more paths I can see that God is leading me down," Elizabeth said.

"God does call us down many paths," Paul agreed. "I see that now."

"I'm glad," Elizabeth said.

"And that's why I bought this buggy," Paul said.

Elizabeth's eyebrows knit together in confusion. "What do you mean?"

"This buggy is big enough for a family," Paul said. "I've been praying about it for a while now, and I felt led to buy it now."

"Paul, what are you saying?" Elizabeth asked as her breath caught in her chest.

"I'm asking if you will marry me," Paul said. Before she could answer, he rushed on, "I know what I said before, but I see now that you being a midwife is what God wants for you right now, and that doesn't take anything away from our marriage, if you'll say yes that is."

Blood pulsed through Elizabeth's veins triple time, and there was a rushing sound in her ears. She had been praying so hard for this very thing, and now that it was happening she knew that she needed to pray. *Lord, please show me what You have planned for me. Amen.*

As Paul reached over to take her other hand, he said, "And I know now that you should deliver babies as long as you can, as long as the Lord wills it. I will never stand in your way again."

That was the answer to her prayer. She opened her eyes wide as tears pooled in the corners, and she whispered, "Yes. I will marry you, Paul."

Paul leaned over to seal their engagement with a kiss, and Elizabeth felt God's peace descend upon her. She was glad that the two of them had gone through this rough patch because now she knew how to listen for God's will in her life. And that was the most valuable thing she could ever hope to learn.

AMISH SUNSET

NANCY MANN

Chapter I

Rain decorated the grassy fields of Lancaster County. The sky was a cloud grey, the sun remaining absent as the county mourned for the loss of William Bradshire, a carpenter that had been known throughout the county for his kindness and love towards the people around him.

Friends and family had gathered in the county's cemetery for William's funeral, one of the mourners being William's love, Mary Lee Warner. Out of everyone there, Mary was the most damaged from it. William's parents had passed on early in his life due to illnesses and the remaining family he had weren't as close. If anything, Mary was the only one there who truly was family to him.

As Bishop David spoke about his memories with William, Mary thought to herself how God could do such a thing, to take away an innocent being this early in his life. William was only in his mid-twenties, like Mary. He had so much to experience in his life, but it was stripped away from him so early due to the accident.

"If anyone has anything to say, speak now." Bishop David said, stepping back and letting anyone step forward to speak.

There was a long pause, silence being present as Mary thought to herself. Eventually, she took a step forward, standing in front of the casket as she let out a depressed sigh.

"William…had a beautiful soul," Mary said quietly, holding onto a wildflower, "a soul that I have yet to find in any other human being."

Everyone was watching her speak, seeing what Mary had in her hand and what she had to say about William being gone.

"I can't imagine not meeting him in my life…all the memories we've made together…all the laughter, the love…I'm going to miss it." Mary spoke as tears ran down her cheeks. "I don't know if I will find another William in my life."

Some of William's family members began to have tears fall too as they listened to Mary's words about their lost kin. Mary soon stepped back from the casket, having finished speaking on the behalf of William's death. Bishop David soon stepped forward again, wiping some tears from his own eyes.

"Thank you Mary…I will say, before I close in prayer, that it will be difficult to find another William in our lives." Bishop David said to Mary before opening his Bible.

Verses from the Bible were soon spoken out loud, everybody bowing their heads in prayer as Bishop David spoke. While everyone listened, Mary wasn't listening to the verses, in fact, she was in her own mind at this point.

"Why God…why would you take William away from me?" Mary thought to herself. *"William didn't even get half way into his life…why would you take him now?"*

As she struggled with the idea of William passing on, Bishop David finished reading the verses, quietly speaking the word *amen* as he closed his Bible, everybody soon leaving the scene of the funeral, letting the casket to be lowered into the grave. While the casket lowered, Mary was the only one present, witnessing her love's final presence on the surface of Earth.

In regards to funeral traditions of the Amish, flowers were not placed on the casket. For Mary though, traditions meant nothing to her in this occasion. She took the wildflower that she was holding in her hand and tossed it down into the undug grave, letting it land on the coffin before the gravediggers began to bury the coffin.

"I love you so much William." Mary said as the coffin soon disappeared from the soil piling on top. Tears continued to fall onto the soil as she left the site of the funeral.

Chapter II

Several years later...the county had returned back to its normal ways, except for Mary. Ever since William passed away, Mary wasn't her old self. Her old cheerful personality had passed on as well, leaving her a closed up, emotionless woman in her mid-twenties.

She tried to return back to a normal life by going to church, seeing if God might be able to help her find peace, but the more she went the church, the more she began to question God. At times, she would find herself being angry at God for taking William away this early in his life. Eventually, Mary stopped going to church, which brought the concern of Bishop David, leading him to go to Mary's home.

Her house was a little way from town, being near one of the farms. She lived in a large house that belonged to William and his parents. Now that William passed on, Mary now owned the house and lived in it by herself.

Bishop David knocked on the front door, waiting for it to be opened. It took a few knocks before the door finally opened, Mary standing there in a stone grey dress.

"Yes?" Mary quietly said, looking at him with her expressionless face.

"May I come in?" Bishop David asked softly, his expression being hopeful that she would accept his request.

Mary let out a quiet sigh before she nodded, stepping out of the way for Bishop David to come in.

"Thank you...Mary." He said, soon walking into her home, looking around.

Mary shut the door behind Bishop David, walking past him and sitting down on a chair in the living room, continuing what she was doing before he knocked. When Bishop David sat down across from her, he noticed that she was knitting a quilt.

"Oh...I see that you've been busy with making a quilt." Bishop David said, giving Mary a gentle smile.

"Quilts. I've been busy making quilts." She said quickly, pointing in the corner to a basket of several quilts.

Bishop David was surprised by the amount of quilts she had made. "That's quite the number of quilts Mary." He said with a small laugh after.

Mary raised her eyebrows as she continued to knit the quilt. "I've found that work is one of the few things that keeps me from thinking about the past." She said softly, not making eye contact with Bishop David.

"Oh...well...if that's what helps you find peace." He said quietly, rubbing the back of his neck before he finally decided to talk about why he wanted to talk to her. "Mary...I'm worried about you."

She heard Bishop David, stopping for a second before she continued knitting the quilt. "Why?" Mary questioned him.

"I'm concerned for you because you haven't been going to church for months." Bishop David finally said, looking at her with a worried expression. "You were always an avid church-goer when William..." He said before realizing what he said, stopping in mid-sentence.

Mary immediately looked up when Bishop David brought up William, her knitting ceasing before she let out a sigh of disbelief escape her lips. She set the quilt and knitting needle down. "Please, do not ever bring up William to me again when comparing me to then and now." Mary said, her voice trembling as she had grown an upset expression.

Bishop David had become silent as he listened to Mary finally speak to him.

"I'm no longer the Mary from then because of the events that happened, and if you want to visit me and tell me how I use to love church and that you're concerned with me not being there on Sundays, then don't even speak, you're wasting your breath." Mary said to him, her eyes staring into his intensely.

Bishop David heard everything she was saying before he let out a sigh of sympathy. "I'm sorry Mary that you're like this...I didn't come here today to chastise you about not attending church. I came here because I'm really concerned for what you've become. I want happiness for you, I want you to have that cheerful personality that everybody knew you for." He said softly, standing up from sitting, looking down at her. "Always remember Mary, we all face events in life that we don't want, but it's all a part of God's plan for something greater."

Mary just glared at him the whole time he spoke, not even acknowledging the things he said. "I would like you to leave."

Bishop David heard her request and nodded softly, walking away from where they were at and leaving the house.

She had watched him leave through the windows before she finally reached for her knitting needles and quilt, continuing to knit as she thought about what he said about God having a plan for everyone. To her, God's plan was killing William and taking away something that she loved most in the world, when she didn't have anyone else.

"Forget God." Mary said to herself quietly, having completely lost faith and love in God.

Chapter III

One stormy night soon had arrived in Lancaster County. Rain had arrived over the town and fields, the sound of sharp pellets hitting the roofs and windows of each building. The window whirled between each building, the sounds of wind wailing could be heard by anyone who was awake.

While the storm stayed present in the county, Mary was asleep in her bed, although she wasn't sleeping soundly. The red-headed woman was having a nightmare, causing her to toss back and forth in her sleep before some sort of sound interrupted her slumber.

KNOCK KNOCK KNOCK

Mary sat right up from her bed like a vampire in a coffin, rubbing her eyes. "What on Earth?" She said to herself, looking around the room as she wondered what caused her to wake up.

KNOCK KNOCK KNOCK

This time, the red-head heard the solution to the noise. "Who could be at my door in the middle of the night?" Mary got out of her bed, wrapping her blanket around herself to cover her nightgown. She made her way down the stairs of her home before seeing the front door. Once she got to the door, she slowly opened it, seeing who it was.

There was a man, about her age, with a young daughter about six-years-old. They were wet from head to toe, shivering as they looked at Mary.

"Please...do you have room in your home for my child and I? We come from far away to Lancaster County...we have no home, no food." The man said, his tone being a desperate one.

Mary had no idea that this was what waited for her on the other side of the door. "I...Well..." She looked at the two before she finally nodded quickly, stepping out of the way.

"Oh thank you...thank you!" The man said happily and emotionally. He quickly moved inside, Mary shutting the door behind the two. Even though they were inside, away from the rain, they still were shivering in the dark home. Mary saw how cold they were and immediately knew what they needed.

She quickly went over to the fireplace in the living room, taking two logs that were on the side of the hearth in a pile and putting them inside the fireplace. After a few attempts of trying to get a fire started, she eventually managed to do so, an orange glow illuminating the living room.

Once the man saw the fire, he moved his daughter close to the fireplace, trying to get her as warm as possible. Mary saw what he was trying to do and quickly went over to the eight-year-old, wrapping her blanket around the child. The man soon began to dry off her daughter while at the same time trying to get her warm.

"There you go...nice and warm now. Away from the cold rain." He said quietly to his daughter, holding her close as he sat in front of the fireplace with her.

The daughter shivered still, but the warmth from the fire and the blanket caused the shivering to decrease as the time went by.

Mary stood behind the two, watching them and making sure that they were okay. "Are you warm enough?" She asked them, having held one of the quilts she had made in her hands to give to the man.

"Yes...thank you kind miss." He said quietly, holding his daughter close before taking the quilt from Mary, wrapping it around himself.

With the two warming themselves up from the fire, Mary decided to grab another quilt for herself before sitting down on her couch. She wrapped the quilt around her body so she could be warm too. Since she now had two "guests" in her home, she didn't want to go upstairs, back to bed, with the knowledge that two strangers were downstairs in her home, two people who she had no idea who they were.

"Maybe they're thieves," Mary thought to herself, studying the two strangers. *"Although...she looks pretty young to be a thief."* She finally decided to speak up, wanting to figure out who they were. "Where did you two come from?"

The man looked back at her, hearing her question before he began to reply to her. "We came from Somerset County." The man answered, still trying to warm up his daughter.

"Oh...that's far from here." Mary replied, sitting down on her couch, looking at the man.

"It very much is..." The man nodded, looking at her. "Do you know if there's any housing here in Lancaster County?"

Mary heard her question before she shrugged. "I'm not too sure. Are you looking for a place to stay?"

The man nodded, looking down at his daughter. She had fallen into slumber and had a warm expression on her face and had stopped shivering, indicating she was no longer freezing. "Yes."

She heard him and asked some more questions in order to get to know him. "Why Lancaster County? I'm sure there's plenty of other settlements along the way."

"I just," The man began to say, rubbing the back of his neck nervously, "I don't know...I guess I've heard a lot of great things about Lancaster. Figured that it would be a great place for my daughter to grow up in."

Mary nodded when he stated that it'd be a good place for his daughter to grow up in. "Lancaster really is a nice place to grow up in...a good place to start a fam-" she began to say before stopping when she was about to say "family." It reminded her of what she has always wanted to have and that made her think of William and her. "Well, it's a good place to meet nice and caring people."

The man saw her reaction when she was talking about family, but decided not to question it in order to remain polite. "That's good to hear...by the way," the man began to say, looking at her once again, "what is your name?"

She heard him and replied softly. "Mary...my name is Mary Lee Warner."

When the man heard her, he smiled softly. "That's a beautiful name."

Mary smiled softly when he complimented her name. "What about you? What's your name?"

"Robert." He said quietly, before looking down at his daughter, gently stroking her hair. "The little one is Miriam."

Chapter IV

The next morning had arrived, the rain was now gone, the only trace of rain being the puddles in the dirt. Mary decided to help Robert and Miriam out by going down to the church to see Bishop David could help them out.

Entering the church, there were only a few people present in the pews, praying to the Lord about whatever comes to their attention. Bishop David was not preaching, considering it was a Tuesday, so chances were he was at his home.

"Doesn't look like he's here." Mary said, turning around and leading Robert and Miriam out.

"Who are we looking for exactly?" Robert said, holding his daughter's hand as they walked towards Bishop David's house.

"We're looking for David, Lancaster County's bishop. He might be able to help you out with moving here." Mary replied, reaching the bishop's house before knocking on the door. Not too long after the knock, the door opened, Bishop David standing there.

"Mary?" He said, a little surprised. "What brings you here today?"

Mary explained the whole story to him, telling the bishop that Robert and Miriam showed up in the middle of the night, needing a place to stay and that they wanted to move to Lancaster.

"I see..." Bishop David said quietly, scratching his beard as he thought about it. "Unfortunately, there isn't any houses available right now."

Mary heard the news and let out a quiet groan. "So where will they stay if they don't have a home?"

Bishop David heard her before looking at the two, looking at Mary again. "Can I talk to you privately Mary?"

Mary was confused as to why, but nodded as she stepped inside the bishop's house. "What did you want to talk to me about?"

Bishop David looked at her before he let out a quiet sigh. "I wanted to talk to you privately about where they're going to stay. I believe they should continue living at your house until a new house can be built here in the county."

She listened to what he said before hearing his statement about the two staying at her home. "What? No. I can't have people living at my house."

Bishop David gave her a confused look. "Why not? You have one of the biggest houses here in Lancaster County. You're not living with anyone. There's plenty of room in the house for someone."

"Because, I don't have enough food to feed two more people. I don't want to start housing people." Mary was quick to say, folding her arms. "I can't let strangers come into my home and make themselves acquainted to the hou-"

"Mary." Bishop David interrupted, clearly showing he was getting irritated with her. "Enough with the excuses. I'm not going to force you to let them in. I'm only suggesting you give the two of them a home. It's not permanent, but where else are they going to go?" He asked Mary, looking at her with a serious expression. "They can't move into anyone else's home. They all have families, rather large ones too."

She listened to him, looking into his eyes as she thought about everything he was saying. Bishop David was right in many ways. Most families in the county had large families, homes that were already crowded. With Mary's house, it was just her. He even said that it wasn't permanent, so it'd be something that Mary didn't have to deal with for too long.

"I guess...I could have them stay for a little while." Mary finally admitted, realizing that she could be a little generous.

"Thank you Mary." Bishop David said before leading her back outside, now facing Robert. "We will discuss adding a house whenever I meet my colleagues. Until we can get a house added to the county, you'll have to stay with Mary for the time being."

Robert listened to what Bishop David said, nodding softly. "Okay, thank you."

Bishop David smiled softly, heading back into the house before closing the door.

Robert and Miriam turned toward Mary, looking at her. "So...are we going to back to the nice lady's house?" Miriam asked her father.

Mary heard her and couldn't help but smile. "Yes...yes you are."

Robert watched the two interact before he couldn't help but smile, seeing this stranger being so nice to his daughter.

"Alright. Let's head back to the house so I can get a room prepped up for you two." Mary said, clapping her hands together when she knew what she needed to do.

Chapter V

A couple of months passed by in Mary's household. The two strangers that had showed up on her doorstep were now friends of hers, having brightened up the household little by little. As Mary got to know Robert, he started feeling more and more comfortable around him, the two even joking around with each other.

With Miriam, she started to look up towards Mary as a mother figure, every now and then the little girl called Mary mom. Mary would hear this and laugh, finding it humorous that Robert's daughter called her mom.

While everyone was getting along just fine, Mary started to remember William again, every time she looked at Robert. There was something about Robert that reminded her of William. It might've been the way he made her laugh or the way he showed kindness to people. Whatever it was, Mary could see William through Robert, which made her think about if she found another William in her life.

It was now 6 PM and Robert and Miriam had finished eating dinner with Mary. When they finished, Robert decided to take Miriam to bed, since she started dozing off during dinner. Once she was in bed, she was out cold.

"She must've been really tired today. Miriam never goes to bed this early." Robert said, walking back into the kitchen. "I don't blame her...she didn't sleep that well last night."

"Oh poor thing." Mary said, cleaning the dishes in the sink. "I hope she rests well tonight."

"She probably will." Robert said, walking over before leaning against the counter. "So...what do you want to do?"

Mary continued to wash the dishes before she stopped, soon looking at him. "What do you mean?"

"Well I mean...Miriam is in bed early. Do you want to go out for a walk?" Robert replied, looking at her and waiting to hear an answer.

She looked at him before looking down at the dishes, thinking about his offer before setting the plates down. "I would enjoy that."

He smiled brightly before he walked out of the kitchen, planning on getting his jacket.

It didn't take long before the two were on an adventure, walking around the county in the early evening. The sky was an vibrant orange, the sun easing itself behind the hills.

"Wow...that's a beautiful sunset." Robert said softly, looking at it.

"It sure is." Mary said quietly, looking at it before she looked at Robert. With the two of them having grown closer, she soon started to think more in regards of making their relationship a bit more than friends. "Can I show you something?"

Robert heard her, turning his head and looking at her before he smiled softly. "Yeah of course."

Mary smiled brightly before leading him into the woods, walking in a certain direction. As for Robert, he wasn't sure where she was taking him, which made him a little nervous. Eventually, the two arrived in a rather large open area in the woods, a grass area that was decorated with wildflowers.

"Wow..." Robert quietly said to himself, stepping forward and starting to walk towards the flowers. "They're beautiful."

Mary stood behind Robert, watching his response before walking with him again. "I know. I love coming to this place. It reminds me of so many happy memories." She said before she began to lay down in the grass, looking at the sky that had become as orange as a Doris Longwing Butterfly's wing.

Robert watched what she did before he followed her actions, lying next to her as the two watched the sky. "You have quite the spot...especially one that you value." He smiled softly, relaxing on the grass.

The two watched the sky for a few, enjoying the time to relax with each other. Eventually, Robert spoke up, a question that had been resonating within him.

"How come you didn't want to let us live with you a few months ago?" He quietly said, still looking at the sky, some clouds gently moving along in the sky.

Mary heard him and gave him a confused look. "What do you mean?"

"You were talking to Bishop David the morning after the rainstorm. You told him that you didn't want anyone staying at the house because you didn't have enough food and didn't want housing people. Part of me though doesn't believe that."

Mary listened to what Robert was saying, her expression staying confused before her expression became more of a look of hesitant.

"There's something more than not enough food and not wanting to house people huh? You don't have to tell me, but just know I'm here if you want to talk." Robert said quietly, wanting to assure that she could trust him.

She listened to what he said before she began biting her own lip, thinking to herself before she let out a quiet sigh. "There is...there's a lot more to it. I think it's fair that you should know."

He heard her response to his question and turned onto his side, looking at her now as she began to speak about what the reason for not wanting anyone to live with her.

"It all has to do with a man I loved...a man named William." Mary said quietly.

Chapter VI

William Bradshire...a carpenter of Lancaster County. Most of the county knew him as the kind man who cared about everyone around him, even the ones who didn't care for him. William was the prime example of what it means to follow Christ's footsteps. He showed a strong love towards God, helped out around his community, showed love towards everyone, taught the youth about the Bible, and that's just the peak of the iceberg.

Sometimes in life though, bad things can occur that change one's life. For William, it was losing his parents at the age of eighteen. With his parents gone, he now owned the house, but that meant nothing to William. For a long time, he had struggled with the fact that his parents were gone, but during this time, he still continued to help people, having put them first before himself.

A great example of William putting others first was one cold, dark night. There was a knock on his door, the knock having echoed the entire silent household. When William opened his front door, he found a shivering girl his age, looking up at him. This girl was Mary.

The young girl had ran away from home, angry at her parents and her peers around her community. She was looking for a place to stay, which was she ended up on William's doorstep, a stranger to him. William was caring enough to immediately let her in; he even allowed her to stay as long as she needed. Even though she could've left any time, she found herself a priceless friendship.

Eventually, as time progressed, the redhead soon fell in love with William, the same happening with the boy. The two ended up revealing their love for each other when they discovered and rested in the grass area in the woods with the wildflowers. Ever since then, they were two peas in a pod.

As time progressed, they became closer and closer, almost being one soul. Mary began helping out in the community with him while developing a strong love of God since William introduced her to Him. Eventually, William decided that he was going to ask Mary for her hand in marriage, but his colleagues asked for his help in finishing the construction of a barn.

Unfortunately, William never had the chance to pop the question due to the accident. While he was watching his colleagues raise one of the barn walls up by pulling it up with ropes, the ropes snapped and the wall soon fell on William, his chances of escaping the wall very low with how fast the whole situation took. Sadly, William didn't survive the heavy barn wall crushing him.

Word soon got out around the county about William dying from the accident, which Mary soon heard about. She was devastated, crushed, her heart torn into pieces for the loss of her one true love.

After William had passed, Mary was given the house, considering she basically lived there and was a member of the community. During this time, Mary closed herself off from the rest of the world, locking herself away in her home, mourning the loss of William. She even decided to not let anyone into the house after the loss in order to keep the house peaceful, like it was when William and her were in it.

Even in the present, Mary still has nightmares about the whole incident, nightmares that remind her of the loss of William.

"If only I were there to stop him...to get him out of the way...If only I were there...he'd still be alive."

Chapter VII

Once Mary finished telling Robert the story, she had developed some tears from the memory of William's death.

"Now you know why I don't let anyone into the house...I know...it sounds insane, for the girlfriend of someone who has departed to keep the house like a temple. You must think I'm crazy..." Mary said quietly, wiping her tears.

"Oh no..." Robert said, looking at her. "I don't think you're insane at all...I can see why you value the house so much. All the memories with William...the laughter...the peace...everything about it...you don't want anyone to ruin this place for you." He said softly, gently resting his hand on hers. "I'm sorry...I didn't know this was the reason why you didn't want us here."

Mary heard him and finally broke down, tears rolling down her cheeks as she covered her face with her hands, muffled crying heard behind it. Robert reached for her and wrapped his arms around her, holding her close as he embraced her.

"Shhh...it's okay...Mary." Robert quietly said, stroking her hair gently to calm her down. "It's okay..."

After years of suppressing the memories of William and her, the pain she has endured from remembering his death, the many tears she had held back, she finally broke down and let her tears flow.

"I miss him so much...every day I wish I could see him again...tell him that I wish I could've saved him from the wall...I wish I could've done something." She said, pressing her face against Robert's shoulder as she shook from her crying.

"You couldn't do anything Mary...you had no idea that would happen..." Robert said softly, continuing to hold her close as she cried against him. "Look on the bright side...with William having a strong love for God, he's finally in Heaven where he can be with God...walk along with him...talk to him...laugh with him."

With Robert's words entering Mary's ears, it made her cry more. He was right in the sense that she wouldn't have known and that he's in a better place now. Her heart ached as she recalled all the memories of William from when they met to his death. All the memories were mainly happy and ones that would make her laugh whenever she looked back to them. Even though William was gone, she remembered one thing...William lives on through her. The memories, the house, the ideology, everything that William was made up of lives on through Mary. With this thought, she felt like she could finally get over the tragedy of losing William and achieve peace.

"Thank you...Robert...Thank you." Mary said quietly, looking up at him with tears in her eyes.

Robert looked down at her, confused as to why she was telling him thank you. "For what?" He laughed gently, wiping the tears away from her eyes.

"For saying all of those things about William and I...I've spent all these years holding onto William's tragedy and blaming myself for not being able to help him, but now I can finally find peace and let go of the tragedy...thank you...Robert." She finally said, looking at him as she gently reached up, stroking his cheek before she finally decided to lean in, kissing him gently.

Robert was caught off guard with the kiss, his eyebrows raising as she held her in his arms. Eventually, she broke the kiss, resting her head on his should. "Let's go back home...it's getting late." Mary said quietly, her eyes now closed.

Even though Robert had thought about pushing their relationship to another level, there was something that was holding him from reaching that level, something that had followed him from his previous home.

Chapter VIII

Many weeks had passed by since Mary told Robert about her past. Mary was in a much brighter mood, slowly building herself up again by socializing with people, going to church again, which made Bishop David happy, and she started wearing colorful clothes again.

Robert was thinking about what Mary had done in the wildflower area in the woods on the porch. He wanted to moved towards the next step, but the past was catching up with him.

"Hey!" Mary called out, coming up to the house with Miriam. "We've got dinner!"

He snapped back into reality, smiling gently when he saw the two. "Oh...that's wonderful. Looks delicious." Robert said, standing up and helping them take the food inside the house.

"I decided to cook something special for you...to thank you for helping me return back to my old self again."

Robert smiled and chuckled nervously, rubbing the back of his neck. "Oh...you don't have to do that."

"But papa," Miriam spoke out, looking at him, "look at the food! It looks delicious! At least let mom...Mary cook it for me."

Both Robert and Mary laughed at Miriam's comment, Mary picking her up and holding her.

"Okay, well if Robert doesn't want his special dinner, then I'll cook it for you." She said, walking in with the child.

"That'd be fantastic!" Miriam exclaimed happily.

Robert followed behind the two with the groceries, his expression being lost in thought as he thought about the past.

Dinner time soon arrived, everyone now seated at the table as they waited for Mary to come in with the special dinner.

"Whatever she's cooking, it smells delicious." Miriam said, excited to eat.

In a matter of minutes, Mary came out with a cooked turkey, the skin being a golden crisp.

Even though Robert wasn't asking for a special dinner, he was impressed with how the turkey came out. "Wow, looks really good Mary."

She smiled brightly, setting the plate down. "Well I'm glad you like it so much. I've got more coming out. I cooked some corn, made so mashed potatoes, have some greens." Mary explained to them as she walked back into the kitchen.

It took a few trips for her before she finally could sit down at the table with the two. "Alright, dig in." Mary said, taking her knife and fork, cutting into the turkey and scooping up a little bit of everything.

The dinner that they had all together was nice. Lots of laughter, lots of compliments, complete joy filled the room between Miriam and Mary, although Robert was most of the time quiet. After dinner, Miriam decided to go play with her doll in the living room while Mary and Robert were in the kitchen, cleaning the dishes.

While they were in there, Robert remained quiet, lost in his thoughts as he kept trying to shake it off. It didn't take too long though for Mary to see something was bothering him.

"You've been awfully quiet this evening...is there something wrong?" Mary asked him, continuing to wash the dishes.

"No." Robert said vaguely, not wanting to get into what was bothering him.

"You sure?" She said softly, looking at him. "You seem like you're thinking really hard about something."

"Don't worry about it." Robert said to her, trying to avoid explaining his thoughts.

Eventually, Mary let out a quiet sigh before setting her dish down, turning toward Robert.

"You know if something is troubling you, you can te-" Mary began to say to him.

"Drop it." Robert said harshly, looking at her for a few quick seconds before he finally set his plate down, shaking his head. "Just forget it...I'm going to bed." He said, leaving the kitchen and walking upstairs.

Mary was shocked by the way Robert reacted, considering it wasn't normal for Robert to be this way.

Miriam heard the commotion from the living room, looking at Mary. "Is papa upset about something?" She said with a concerned voice.

Mary heard Miriam and shook her head. "Don't worry about it dear. He just needs some time to himself."

Chapter IX

Robert currently laid in Mary's bed upstairs, his eyes closed as he tried sleeping. He didn't mean to snap at Mary, but considering his thoughts were getting to him, it was bound to happen. As he attempted to sleep, he soon felt something lay next to him, which interrupted his slumber. He opened his eyes and turned to look and see if it was Mary.

Of course, he was right in this situation. Mary was in her nightgown, having crawled in bed with Robert, getting cozy. Once he saw it was Mary, he returned back to his previous position, his back facing her. Still trying to avoid breaking the news to Mary, he soon felt her arms around his stomach, her body soon pressing against his back.

"What's going on with you? You're usually not like this." She said softly, resting her head against his back.

"I don't know Mary...I don't know." Robert said quietly, his eyes still closed.

"I feel like you do know Robert." Mary finally said. "I just feel like you don't want to tell me what you're thinking of."

He heard what she said, but didn't reply to it. The only thing he did was sit in silence with his eyes closed, trying to fall into slumber.

"You know I'm here if you want to tell me what's bothering you. I think it'd be healthy if you did though because you won't get any sleep with you thinking about whatever you're thinking. I know from experience." Mary quietly said, now closing her eyes as she rested her head against his back.

Robert listened to what she was saying before he let out a quiet sigh, trying to think about how he would explain his thoughts to her. Eventually, he decided to be straightforward with her.

"You know why I decided to move to Lancaster County?" He asked Mary quietly.

She merely shook her head against his back, indicating that she didn't know why he moved here. "Aside from finding a new home, no I don't."

Robert listened to what she had to say before he continued. "I left my previous home because my wife walked out on Miriam and I."

When Mary heard this, her eyes opened up and she sat up, looking down at him. "What? That's horrible! Why would she do that?"

Once Mary sat up, Robert turned so that he was laying on his back, now looking up at her. "To be honest...maybe I married the wrong person. She just...everything seemed fine to me. She was a good mother, I was a good father, we lived a happy life, but then one day..." He said before stopping, thinking back to that day before telling Mary what happened.

———

"Sara?" He called out, looking around his home. "Where are you?

While he walked around the house, Miriam watched him, not understanding what was going on. "Papa? What's going on?"

"I can't find mom. She's gone." Robert said, his tone being a little more scared. "Maybe she left something saying where she went. Yeah...she leaves notes."

"Maybe...I'll help you try and find something" Miriam said, getting off of the couch before walking around their home, trying find anything that could lead to the mystery of where Robert's wife went.

Eventually, Miriam found a note that had fallen on the side of the bed. "Papa!" She called out. "I found a note!"

Robert immediately ran into the room, seeing the note in Miriam's hand. He took the note from her and began reading it. Although the hope he had on his expression when he found the note soon faded the more he continued to read it. In fact, he soon had become emotionless from what was written on the note.

"What does it say papa?" Miriam asked, looking up at him.

Robert finished reading the note, looking down at Miriam before folding the note in half, tucking it into his pocket. "Don't worry about it sweetheart. I think though...we need to move away from this county."

When Miriam heard this, she was completely confused. "Why? Why do we need to move?"

He heard her before he picked her up, looking around the house one last time. "Because I think we will find somewhere else that'll be better for the both of us."

"We basically left the county with nothing but the clothes on our back. I couldn't stand living in the same county as her and live in a house that we lived in together." Robert said quietly, looking at Mary as he finished explaining his story. "Would you stay in the same place if you found out your love left you and your child for someone else?"

When Mary heard this, she let out a depressed sigh. "No...I don't think I would." She said quietly. "Is that what's been on your mind today?"

Robert heard her before nodding softly. "I've been thinking about it for a long time now...I've wanted to move onto the next step in our relationship, but...I fear that something would happen again...I fear the odds of you walking out on us."

Once Robert said that, Mary spoke up in a more serious tone. "Robert...look at me."

Robert did as told and look into her eyes, seeing what she would say.

"I would never do that...ever in my life." Mary said, looking at him as she gently rested her hand on his cheek. "I wouldn't do something to hurt you and Miriam...I love you both, with all my heart." She said to him before she gently kissed him, breaking it soon after before resting her head on his chest. "You don't need to worry about me every walking out on you two...I care about you two so much that my heart aches. I wouldn't even think about walking out on you two."

When Robert heard this, he let out a relieved sigh, his arms wrapping around her and hugging her against him. "I love you so much Mary..."

"I love you too Robert..."

Tears of an Amish Widow

Erica Hennig

There were a lot of things in life that Hannah King imagined she'd be. A mother, a wife, possibly even a mentor to young women; a widow was not something she'd imagined for herself.

There was an illness running through the little Plain community. It was something like pneumonia, but the English doctors were having a hard time controlling it as well. Hannah's husband, Joab, was a farmer with a caring heart. He chose to follow the doctor around and help him however he could. Since the illness was contagious, Joab eventually became sick.

Hannah wasn't going to let this illness stay in the community anymore. She made the decision to take Joab to the actual English hospital. Though they were able to keep him alive a little longer, they still could not save Joab. Hannah was crushed, her heart felt as though it had been ripped out of her chest and beaten with a sledgehammer over and over.

How am I going to take care of our little Samuel? How will I live? Who will take care of me?

The oncoming depression wasn't one she could push away with a few good thoughts and a well-placed Bible verse. She desperately tried praying, hoping that the God she served would send a sign that everything would be alright... but nothing came. No signs in the sky, no angels to comfort, and no one to care for her and her little boy.

Ultimately, she knew that the community would take care of her for a time, but she also knew that she would have to pull herself together eventually. Especially if she was going to continue to support her son. He no longer had a father, and Hannah was determined to make sure he had a mother.

Day in and day out, she began to do what she could to care for Samuel. She worked in the local store, and sold things she knitted at the market on the weekends. Hannah would help in the schoolhouse if they let her, and they did until Samuel got to be the age that he could go to school. The community leaders decided having one of the students' parents there would cause a conflict in the community as to why a certain parent was allowed there and none others.

Just as the new school year was around the corner, the school teacher—Miss Schwartz—got married and decided to quit teaching. Hannah didn't understand how the community could let something like that happen. She went on a rampage one day and told the leaders exactly what she thought of them in the little church building where they were meeting.

"How could you leave the children with no one? Who in this community will train our children on the right path? You must have *something* in place! Surely, you're not that stupid."

She heard a throat clear behind her and saw a handsome, young man standing in the doorway. He smiled as her face flushed with embarrassment.

"Ms. King, this is Michael Fisher," one of the elders said. "He will be the new school teacher. We have decided that you will assist him for the first three weeks of classes, then you must find something else to occupy your time."

"'Occupy my time?' You make teaching sound like a hobby! Isn't investing in the next generation important to you?" Hannah felt a hand on her shoulder and she knew it was the new guy, Michael. Something about his touch calmed her, and her heart instantly ached for the tender touch of a husband again.

"Ms. King," Michael's voice was barely above a whisper. "Let them do what they feel is right. I care about the children just as much as you do. We'll work something out for you."

Hannah relaxed a little, nodded in response, then turned around and walked out of the church. She discovered that the men in that room might not have cared for the children, but the man taking over as school teacher certainly did. And she could get behind a man that was confident in what he was doing. She was going to make the next three weeks the most meaningful yet.

Samuel was so excited for the first day of school that he could hardly contain himself. Hannah walked with him a little earlier than most other students. She wanted to be there early to make a better impression than the first time for Michael.

He probably won't even remember me anyway, she thought to herself. *Almost every single girl in the community has made contact with him. I'm sure we've all started to look the same to him.* Though Hannah was afraid to admit what exactly that meant, even to herself. She hated lumping herself in with all of the young, unmarried girls in the community, but sometimes she found herself acting just like them. Of course it was only a few years ago that she was unmarried and pining for every guy that walked into her life.

Her train of thought was interrupted by Samuel suddenly dashing off toward the school.

"Samuel, wait!"

Hannah tried to call him back or catch up with him, but he had such a head start that he was in the school building before she had even crested the hill the school was standing on. Michael popped his head out of the door, probably looking for the parents of the small child who had just entered the school an entire hour before school was even to start. As soon as he saw Hannah, he smiled wide.

"Ms. King," he declared instantly.

So much for forgetting who I am, she thought as her face grew warm.

"Mr. Fisher," she spoke politely. "I just want to apologize for the way we met—"

Michael held his hand up. "No need. All is forgiven. And please, call me Michael."

"Hannah." She stuck out her hand for him to shake, but he took it and kissed it lightly instead. Her heart skipped a beat.

"The pleasure is mine," he said as he looked into her eyes. His were a deep green that fit well with the sandy blond hair on his head and tan skin she could see. Hannah thought he looked almost too tan to be a teacher, but decided the first official meeting wasn't the right time to bring that up.

"Samuel and I are here early to help you set up since it's the first day of school," Hannah quickly changed the subject before her mind went any further away from the original reason she was there so early.

Michael turned and walked into the building, ready to have a helper there.

"I'm glad you'll be here for a few weeks. Sometimes the first three weeks are the hardest on a teacher."

"You've taught before?" Samuel sounded surprised. Michael laughed.

"Of course, buddy," Michael bent down to Samuel's level and addressed him directly. "I was a teacher in another community before I came here."

"Why didn't you stay there then?"

"Because I heard there was another town that needed help, and I like a good hero story." Michael winked as Samuel's eyes grew wide.

Hannah laughed at the exchange before telling Samuel to make sure that every desk had pencils.

As the boy ran off, Hannah began to explain to Michael what they had done last year before Michael cut her off with a wave of his hand.

"I do appreciate the input Hannah, but I would like to do something a little different this time. The children don't know me, and I don't know any of them. I don't want to really come down as an overbearing teacher on my first day." Michael winked. Hannah didn't understand that logic, and she certainly didn't appreciate feeling like she was being spoken to condescendingly.

"Excuse me, sir, but I think we should at least address what the children did." Hannah was going to let him have it anyway. "The children come here to learn, not to make friends with the teacher. If you think for one second I'll let you get away with talking to me like that, you have some life choices to reevaluate." Michael's eyebrows shot up, but he didn't say anything.

Hannah continued. "You might think you're some big hot shot coming here on the invitation of the elders, but you're only here because I already have a child and they won't let parents of a child in the school be the teacher. So you can take the smug, entitled attitude and stick it... somewhere!" She turned and walked out of the building, now feeling like a bit of a moron for telling the handsome, new school teacher off. She was only outside a few minutes before Samuel came and got her.

"Mama, don't let Mr. Fisher scare you away," he spoke tenderly to her. "Besides, maybe he can help you become an even better hero." Hannah looked at her son and realized that even though she didn't think very highly of herself, he thought the world of her. And she wasn't going to let him down; not today, and not ever.

"Okay," she consented as she gave Samuel a hug. "Let's go inside and show him how it's done."

The next few week flew by quickly, and the fact that Michael had been making subtle advances wasn't lost on Hannah. She loved the fact that someone was even toying with the idea of courting her. Since it had been almost five years since Joab had passed on, Hannah didn't think any man would ever take a liking to a woman with a child.

There was only a small problem with the whole situation, and Hannah hated to admit it to herself. Abigail Miller had also shown an interest in the young Mr. Fisher. She was by far the prettiest girl in town with her beautiful blonde hair, deep blue eyes and nearly flawless skin. There wasn't much wrong with Abigail, except that if she didn't get her way she tended to have a fit. But with all of the guys in town constantly pining for her, that rarely happened. Until Michael Fisher came along.

Hannah wasn't sure if he was declining young Abigail's advances or simply playing hard to get, but it made Hannah a little nervous. She felt like there might have been something between them, but this was the last day that she would see Michael on a regular basis. Since it wasn't out of the realm of normal things she would do, she had already decided that she would walk Samuel home from school everyday. Especially if that meant she got to see Michael Fisher for a few minutes.

As all of the children were released to go home, Hannah decided to see if she could get an idea of what was going on in his head.

"This is my last day," she picked up a pencil off the floor as if it was the only purpose she had in the world. She looked up at Michael at the front of the room. He simply nodded, his face tight with emotion.

"Are you okay?" Suddenly nothing else mattered. She moved to the front of the room and stood next to him.

"I just hate it that things have to come to an end," he began to cry. Hannah was shocked. She'd never really seen a grown man cry before, and she wasn't sure what to do. She put her hand on his arm.

"How can I help you?"

"You can stay," he chuckled. They both knew that wasn't her decision and she said as much. Michael replied, "That doesn't mean you can't try to get an extension."

"I'm a woman," Hannah shot back. "They are far less likely to listen to me than they are to you. Besides, you're the teacher. You know what you need far better than I do."

"All I need is you."

Hannah froze. Did she just hear him correctly? "What?"

He pulled away. "You're right, I shouldn't have said that. I apologize." He began busying himself with unnecessary papers on the desk.

"Michael." Hannah grabbed his arm and he stopped. He looked at her and their eyes met. Tears were brimming in his eyes. She wanted to hear him say it again. "What did you say?"

"All I need is you." He turned to face her fully. Her heartbeat sped up, but her breathing became shallow. She knew this feeling; Joab used to make her feel this way. But Joab was gone, so she attempted to push all thoughts of her dead husband out of her mind.

Michael looked at her a moment longer, but he must have seen the inner turmoil because he finally said, "No." And he turned and went back to the useless straightening.

"Did I do something wrong?" Hannah's heart hurt a little as she was suddenly treated very coldly. He stopped.

"No, but I need to take this slowly. Not for your sake, but for mine. There's so much I haven't been able to tell you because we've been at school. Let's have dinner tonight. Bring Samuel. The Miller's live right next door and they have a son he can play with."

Hannah knew the Miller's well, especially because Abigail was the one after Michael's heart. This was a good sign though, because it meant that although Abigail was trying, she wasn't doing as well as she might have thought. And she wasn't asked over for dinner like Hannah. She would still be careful not to give in too much to this. There had been too many times already where men thought they wanted Hannah, but they didn't want Samuel. Since the pair were a package deal, there wasn't much option once they realized how serious Hannah was about her son.

I guess we'll find out tonight how he really feels.

As he usually was, Samuel was ecstatic to be spending any time with Mr. Fisher.

"Do we need to bring anything, Mama? I can't imagine that a *man* would cook anything well." Samuel made a face as he finished his thought. Hannah laughed.

"Samuel, don't be so mean," she playfully scolded him. "Maybe he had all sisters and learned how to cook from them. Maybe he was an only child. I don't know, but you can ask him when we get there."

The ten-minute walk seemed to be the longest walk of their lives. As they got closer, Samuel got more talkative, but Hannah became more quiet. *What if he decides he doesn't like me? How will I tell Samuel?*

Does he even like Samuel? It seems as though he likes children, but sometimes Samuel is a handful. Maybe we should turn around...

The doubting game was becoming too much. Hannah felt a hand wrap around her hand and looked down to find her son had grasped her and was smiling up at her.

"Remember Mama," Samuel said sweetly. "No matter what this man thinks of you, I still love you." She felt an unchecked tear slide down her cheek. She stopped and scooped the little boy into her arms, as they held each other and cried. When Hannah finally put Samuel down he said, "Besides, Jesus still loves you too. And He's the only man you need that *really* matters."

Hannah had to keep from crying because they had already rounded the corner onto the street where Michael lived and he was standing in the doorway waiting for them. Hannah began to apologize for keeping him waiting, but he just waved his hand as he usually did when he didn't want to hear excuses.

"Anything you need to say isn't going to make up for the lost time, so let's not waste any more with apologies." He smiled as if to say there was no need to feel bad for anything she did, though she still felt the need to apologize for apologizing before realizing that would have been counterproductive. She stepped over the threshhold behind her son and was surprised to see an almost immaculate house with the smell of roast beef, carrots and potatoes wafting throughout.

"Mama, it doesn't smell this good when you cook!" Samuel seemed to suddenly have no filter. Thankfully, Michael took it gracefully and defended Hannah's honor.

"Now now, that's not what we say to our mother, is it?" He knelt to Samuel's level, ever the teacher. "She cooks for you, doesn't she?"

The little boy nodded.

"You're never hungry, are you?"

He shook his head.

"Do you sleep in a house?"

A nod.

"Do you have decent clothes to wear?"

Another nod.

"How about some nice shoes?"

One more nod for good measure.

"Then you only say nice things about the woman that treats you well."

"Yes sir," Samuel said before Michael nodded and stood.

"Now," he clapped his hands together. "Who's ready for dinner?"

During dinner, Samuel asked every question he said he was going to, from how he knows how to cook to why is his house so clean to why does he teach. Everything seemed to be going really well until suddenly the 5-year-old had a different plan for the interrogation.

"Do you plan on marrying Mama?"

Hannah's face quickly grew warm and she studied the plate in front of her, afraid of what Michael would say. *This wasn't supposed to happen!*

Without skipping a beat, Michael replied, "Well, that really depends on her. I've already made my decision, but if she keeps pushing me away... then we'll see."

"That would be really stinky. Because Mama really likes you and she's a lot happier with you in her life. In fact, I don't think I've ever seen her this happy. She even sings in her sleep now." Michael laughed at the boy's sudden burst of random facts.

"Oh, does she?" Samuel wasn't even phased.

"Yeah. I think they're songs she used to sing with Papa, but I was a baby when he died, so I only hear stories now. But I think she told me once that was a song she used to sing with him." Samuel shrugged before adding, "Do you have anything for dessert?"

"As a matter of fact I do. Then, you should go play with David Miller next door while you Mama and I talk about grown up stuff."

Samuel seemed to like that idea, so Michael went to get the dessert. Strawberry shortcake with vanilla ice cream.

"Where did you learn how to make ice cream?" Hannah tried to keep the conversation away from their relationship for the time being. She was still reeling from the question of marriage.

"Oh that's simple stuff really... I just went to the English store in town." They all laughed. "More accurately, I have a Mennonite friend who gives me ice cream on a regular basis. It's a treat for me and not one I share with everyone. Tonight, I have two honored guests in my home and I want you both to know that you're special to me."

It was quiet for a few moments, but finally Samuel pushed his chair back and got up from the table without asking.

"I think that was my cue to leave." With that, he walked out the front door and closed it behind him.

"I can't argue with his logic, even if he didn't ask to be excused." Michael looked at Hannah and began his thought. "I've been meaning to tell you this since I met you, but I really do have intentions of marrying you... but like I told Samuel, that is entirely up to you." He sighed and leaned back in his chair. "Would you like to move to the living room? The dishes can wait until later."

Hannah was so enamored by the way Michael's house looked that she couldn't imagine that he was actually fine with leaving dishes unwashed, but she didn't argue because she knew this was a conversation they needed to have.

Once they sat down and were comfortable, Michael continued his thought.

"There is no one in this world who has made me feel more comfortable than you have. From the second I heard how passionate you were about the children until I saw you and Samuel walking up to my house with red eyes from crying, and right up until this moment; there is no one in the world I want in my life more than you and Samuel." He smiled when he said her son's name.

"Who named him?" Michael asked.

"Joab did. He was sick when Samuel was born and said that I was to dedicate him to the Lord just like Hannah did in the Bible."

"Were you having trouble conceiving as well? Actually, I'm sorry—"

Hannah laughed. "No apologies needed, and no we weren't. But he knew from the start that he probably wasn't going to make it. In some ways, it made his passing easier, but in others... it just became harder."

They were quiet for a few minutes before Michael reached out and grabbed Hannah's hand in both of his.

"No matter what anyone says or what anyone does, I will always be here and I will always make my way back to you if you ever feel like we're too far apart."

Hannah had tears in her eyes and she didn't know what to think. The only thing she could manage to get out was, "Why me?"

Michael smiled.

"Because you're everything I've asked God for in a wife, and Samuel is everything I ever wanted in a son."

"What about Abigail Miller? I thought she was interested in you." Hannah simply had to know. She didn't want there to be anymore confusion or dissension between her and the Miller's.

Michael simply shook his head. "She's okay as a person and very beautiful. But she's no Hannah King. You tend to doubt yourself, but you're more beautiful than ten Abigail Millers'. You have beautiful brown hair that reminds me of dark chocolate and rich brown eyes to match. You have cute freckles on your nose that almost seem to contract when you squint your eyes just right... and when you get embarrassed or upset, your face gets really red and it's actually kind of cute." He winked at her.

Despite the tears, she managed to laugh at the last part. She didn't know if she should be rejoicing for herself or praying for Abigail. She loved Abigail like a little sister and would rather have her happy. As if

Michael could suddenly read her mind, he pulled his hands away and gave an exasperated sigh.

"Hannah, Hannah. Why can't you just take the gift that God is giving you? Stop pushing His free love away and stop pushing me away. I'm not usually one to give ultimatums, but if you can't make up your mind, then maybe we shouldn't even try." With that, Michael stood up and went to the kitchen to finish washing the dishes. As he left the living room he called back, "When you're done in there, go ahead and let yourself out. Thank you for coming over."

It was at that moment that Hannah realized she had just potentially thrown her life away. She couldn't move from her spot as much as she didn't want to be there anymore, but she had to do something. So she got down on her knees and just began crying out to the Lord for all of the things she had done to push the people in her life away. She had never done this before, and it was weird to do it in a place that wasn't even familiar, but she knew she needed to do it and she didn't care who could see her.

She didn't know how long she was there for, but when she opened up her eyes and wiped the tears away, she noticed that both Samuel and Michael were on their faces as well, crying and praying along with her. Michael was closest to her, so she put her hand on his back. He began to shake and sob even louder.

When he finally quieted down, she put her mouth down by his ear and whispered, "All I want is you, Michael. I give myself to you."

He breathed a heavy sigh and finally forced himself up. They looked into each other's eyes and knew this was only the beginning of something much deeper than either of them could fathom. He smiled a crooked smile as Samuel sat up with tears still streaming down his face.

"Geez, if you wanted a revival meeting, why didn't you just set one up with the elders?"

Two days later was Sunday, and the town went to church as usual. Michael grabbed Hannah and Samuel on their way out and asked them to stay a few more minutes with him.

"I have something I want to say to the elders and I want you to be there when I do."

"Both of us?" Hannah asked curiously.

"Of course. You come as the whole package." He smiled at them and Samuel couldn't contain his excitement over the mysterious way Michael was acting.

As soon as the last of the churchgoers had left and there were only the elders and the trio, Michael made his move.

"Excuse me, I have something I would like to propose."

The elders looked at him curiously and the preacher said, "Go on."

"I would like for Hannah to be my assistant for the rest of the school year. I know you told her that she couldn't, but the rule that she would be partial to her son is a little silly, since I've seen her in action and she's only more strict on him. These last three weeks have been a huge transition into a position I've never really had before, and Hannah has made everything I've done seem like it was extremely easy."

"We will consider your request, but we can't make any promises," the preacher seemed to be the speaker of the elders today.

"There's also another thing that you might want to consider," Michael seemed to be struggling with this one a little more. He looked at Hannah for just a moment and she nodded, not knowing what he was going to say but showing her support in whatever was about to happen.

"I want to marry her too."

The elders went into a tizzy trying to wrap their heads around this proclamation.

"What? You want to marry a widow?"

"What about children of your own?"

"What about Abigail Miller? Surely she's the better fit."

All of these quick suggestions cut Hannah's heart like a knife, but Michael stopped them all with a wave of his hand.

"My mind's been made up. I love Hannah King and have since I watched her stand up to you almost four weeks ago. And I love Samuel. He's dedicated his life for God's use only and he's everything I always prayed I would have in a son. As for Abigail, God will give her the right man at the right time. I'm not that man, and this is not that time."

The elders simply couldn't believe what they were hearing, but suddenly decided they needed to act right then. They quickly shuffled out of the sanctuary into a back room to discuss, leaving Michael, Hannah, and Samuel alone.

Hannah started to feel those doubts come in again, but this time she stopped them before they could start. *I have a man for the first time in years that loves me like God loves me! How can I ever say no to that kind of love?*

Samuel was starting to get anxious, but Michael wouldn't let him leave, so they began playing a game of tag in the sanctuary. Hannah sat and watched them play, laughing at the way Michael looked, behaving like a 5-year-old.

After almost an hour, the elders finally emerged from the back room. Some of them looked overjoyed and others looked pensive. Hannah wasn't sure if that was a good sign, but she braced her heart for anything.

"Don't." Michael had come up behind her and must have seen her body language. "Don't close your heart. Open it up. Allow yourself to feel. How can you love if you don't let yourself get hurt once in awhile?"

Hannah wasn't sure how to answer that question, but she didn't have the time. Samuel abruptly stopped gallivanting and returned to his place by his mother's side.

The preacher spoke. "We have considered your requests and have but one condition." He looked at the three of them equally. "That you must stay in this town for the rest of your lives and give your lives to serving the children of this community. They need people with big hearts like yours, and this town needs people with new hope to bring a fresh perspective."

"Wait, I have to stay here for the rest of my life?" Samuel asked. "Can't I go home?"

They all laughed as Michael explained he had to stay in the town, not in the church itself. "Ooohhh. Cool!"

Hannah was in shock that they were actually letting this happen. "You're okay with us getting married?"

"God has ordained every man, a wife." The preacher submitted. "And God has ordained every woman, a husband. You have been blessed enough to have been ordained two husbands. The favor of God is on your life, child. We know you won't do anything that would hurt us with it."

Michael pulled her into a hug, as he was still in shock that they said yes. He began to cry into her hair as she cried into his chest. They were going to get to start fresh on everything. And it was the best feeling ever.

Abigail still came to the school everyday to see Michael. Maybe she was hoping she could change his mind, because by now the whole town knew that Michael and Hannah were courting to be married. By the end of that first week, Hannah finally pulled Abigail aside and asked her what was going on.

"I just can't believe that a handsome man like Michael would fall for a widow like you."

Hannah did all she could not to choke the woman out with a bunch of children still around. She wanted to be a good example.

"Well, my dear, I'm sorry that you didn't get your way this time. I guess when it comes to matters of the heart, you're just not the expert."

Abigail huffed, "Who made you the judge on what I'm expert in?"

"Well I know good wife material when I see it, honey. If you want I can help you hone that passion a little better so that people start to take you more seriously. Men like a woman that can really stand up for herself without looking like a 5-year-old."

Abigail looked as if she'd been accosted, but she gathered her composure enough to curtly say, "Maybe I would like that."

Hannah smiled, hoping for only the best in this situation. "Alright then. I'll see you tonight at my house."

"Tonight?"

"Yes. If you want a husband, we must start right away."

"No, I can't do tonight! I have plans."

"With?"

Abigail suddenly looked very flustered. "Someone."

Hannah's eyebrows shot up. "A boy?"

"It's none of your business!" And she picked up the dress from around her heels and marched down the hill.

"What was that all about?" Michael asked as Hannah came back in to finish getting the room ready for tomorrow.

"Abigail's been seeing someone, but she's been coming up here everyday for you. I was nice, but I basically told her she needed to stop."

"I never heard you use those words. It actually sounded as if you were genuinely interested in her life."

Hannah smiled. "It's not like I'm not. I still want to see her do well, even though in her eyes I stole the man she wanted."

Michael stopped what he was doing and pulled her into him. "Hey." He looked deep into her eyes until it felt like he was seeing into her soul.

"No one stole me from anyone. I am my own person and I make my own decisions. Take those thoughts out of your mind right now."

Hannah closed her eyes to clear her head. Suddenly she felt something on her lips. She opened her eyes and saw that Michael was kissing her! She instinctively pulled back and it shocked him.

"What's wrong?"

"Let's... do that again."

This time she was prepared. And it was a glorious kiss with so much emotion and passion behind it. Hannah wasn't sure what had happened last Friday when they were on the floor of his living room, but since then their relationship seemed to be on a fast-track. It was overwhelming at times, but in times like this it felt just right. This was the healing that she needed after Joab died.

As Michael pulled away from Hannah and they looked at each other again, she told him, "Just now was the first time I've thought of Joab in a longing way in a week. Should I feel bad about that?"

Michael shook his head. "The memories of those we loved will always be there, but we have to learn to move on. Thinking of Joab in a longing way meant that even while I was trying to make a move, you were shutting me out. And you did. Now that you've experienced some healing and given a lot of that hurt to God, there's room in your heart to love again."

He suddenly became very serious as he got down on one knee and pulled a small box out of his pocket. He opened it as he spoke to reveal a gold ring with a small diamond set in it.

"With this ring I want you to promise me that you will always be open and vulnerable to me about what's going on. That you will tell me when you're hurting and that you'll tell me when we can rejoice together."

She nodded, too overwhelmed to speak. Her vision became cloudy as he finished his speech.

"As I give you this ring, I promise that I will always protect you and lead you in the ways that God is showing me to take. I promise that I will love and care for Samuel as my own and that he will be my own son... just as you will be my own wife."

Hannah managed to squeak out a "yes" as she threw her arms around her beloved Michael and they cried.

"I love you, my crying widow." They both laughed through the tears as they knew this would certainly not be the last time they cried together.

Their foundation was built solidly on the passion of teaching children and leading each other into the deeper things of God. Hannah knew that this was the best way to start any marriage, and she was blessed to get a second chance to do it all again. This time, she knew it would be for eternity.

When Amish Love Finds A Way

Stephanie Swift

"Katherine, for the love of all things holy and good, will you please stop?"

Katherine Mills sat upright on the church pew and furrowed a brow at her younger brother, Jonah. The worship service would be starting soon, but she couldn't concentrate after discovering one of the buttons on Jonah's shirt was missing. She turned his wrist over to inspect the cuff...again.

"Why didn't you mention it this morning?" she whispered. "I could've mended it before we left."

Jonah jerked his arm from her grasp as his eyes roamed over the congregation. An elderly woman seated in front of them passed a snide glance their way, but the old gossipmonger was the least of her concern.

"Katherine, I'm not a kid anymore. It can wait. Now please stop embarrassing me."

Katherine laced her fingers together on top of her lap and turned her attention to Bishop Abram, who was slowly making his way to the podium at the front of the sanctuary. Her embarrassing Jonah? The thought nearly made her laugh out loud. Oh please...as if he didn't do an excellent job of that on his own. Katherine rolled her eyes heavenward when she caught him winking at a couple of single women sitting on the opposite side of the church.

"Really, Jonah, don't you have any manners?"

He chuckled at her remark before the Bishop garnered the congregation's attention. A hush fell over the crowd and they all bowed their heads when he started the service with a long prayer. She made a mental note to mend Jonah's shirt as soon as they returned home. Perhaps he didn't mind going out in public with tattered clothing, but it bothered her to no end. The last thing she wanted or needed was for the people in their little Amish village to think she was slacking in caring for her brother, a job she'd taken very seriously since their parents' death three years prior.

When Katherine opened her eyes, she was surprised to see someone had joined Bishop Abram behind the podium, but it was no ordinary person, and the stranger certainly wasn't from their community. The gentleman standing beside the Bishop was dressed in English clothing, sporting a short beard and mustache, and he held a cell phone in his right hand. Katherine felt her cheeks flush, and she tried not to stare, but he was quite handsome.

The congregation shared curious glances as the Bishop gestured to the man and introduced him as Dr. Steven Read, a newcomer to Lancaster, but no foreigner to the Amish. He explained how the doctor was raised in the faith as a child in western Pennsylvania, and that he'd discovered his calling in life during his Rumspringa when he was just sixteen years old. He'd practiced medicine ever since and had recently taken over Lancaster's small medical clinic after the previous owner retired from the field.

"My brothers and sisters, I hope you will join me in welcoming Dr. Read to Lancaster and to our community. Several of you have mentioned to me how time-consuming it is to make the trip to the clinic, and Dr. Read has generously volunteered to make house calls."

The excitement in the room was almost palpable and Katherine felt her stomach flutter with excitement also. She'd lost count of the numerous times she'd wrangled Jonah into their carriage and made the long drive to the clinic - sometimes in the dead of night and even during torrential downpours. As far as she knew, the previous doctor never made house calls, at least not to the Amish households, so this was a welcomed change for sure.

After the Bishop introduced Dr. Read and concluded his discussion over the services he would provide, Katherine expected the doctor to leave, but he didn't. Instead, he sat down on one of the front pews and joined in the service. A couple of hours later, when Bishop Abram asked if he'd like to close the service with a prayer, he didn't falter or try to beg his way out of it. He wholeheartedly accepted, and his prayer even received a rousing "amen" from the Bishop when he finished.

Katherine struggled in vain to keep from ogling him, but she couldn't help herself. There was something oddly fascinating about the man - and it wasn't just his rugged good looks either.

"Really, Katherine, don't you have any manners? Stop staring." Jonah mimicked as they stood to leave. Her cheeks burned a bright shade of red as she playfully elbowed him in the stomach, which made him laugh. Two of his close friends caught his attention as they waved to him from across the crowded room, and when he left her side to join them, she was grateful for the reprieve.

Bishop Abram and the doctor stood by the front door, and as Katherine watched him smile and introduce himself to each member of the congregation, she stole a glance toward the back door of the church. Unfortunately, the throng of people was too big to push through so a hasty retreat in the opposite direction wasn't possible.

"Dr. Read, this is Katherine Mills. She and her younger brother, Jonah, own and operate the local dairy farm."

Katherine jerked her head around, not realizing the fast-moving crowd had already nudged her to the front of the line. When she nearly bumped into the doctor, she took a couple of hesitant steps backward to regain her footing.

"H-hello. It's nice meeting you. Welcome to Lancaster," she stammered.

The doctor grinned and thanked her, and Katherine felt her heartrate escalate when the masculine aroma of his cologne wafted past her nose and left her temporarily dazed. He pulled a business card from his jacket pocket and handed it to her, and when their fingers touched, she held her breath.

"Please don't hesitate to call me anytime you have an emergency - day or night," he remarked.

She didn't trust herself to say anything else without sounding like an enamored schoolgirl, so she simply nodded before turning to leave. Perhaps it was just wishful thinking, but she could almost feel the doctors gaze on her as she walked away, which made her legs wobbly and sent a chill up her spine.

Katherine sighed.

She couldn't deny it. The new doctor in town had her spellbound.

* * * *

Steven squinted as he peered out his car window, trying to discern which of the small houses belonged to Miss Hannah Bowen. He glanced at his notepad again and mumbled the information he'd hastily scribbled down while rushing out the door of his clinic.

"House #142. Okay...where are you?"

It was his first medical call to the small Amish village since Bishop Abram introduced him to everyone the previous Sunday, and his stomach flip-flopped with equal parts excitement and fear. He wanted to make a good impression, but as he circled back for what felt like the hundredth time, he started to wonder if he may have bitten off more than he could chew. With the sun setting on the horizon, most of the houses looked identical in the fading light, from their brown tin roofs straight down to the white wooden swings on their front porches.

He strongly considered throwing in the towel until he caught sight of an older woman standing on some porch steps, waving her arms high in the air to get his attention. As he brought his car to a stop in front of the house, he caught sight of the small metallic numbers nailed to one of the porch columns - #142. When he turned off the ignition and stepped out with his medical bag in tow, the woman left the steps and walked around the vehicle to greet him.

"Miss Bowen?" he inquired.

She nodded and motioned toward the front door. "*Yah*, thank you so much for coming, Dr. Read. My son, William, woke up this morning with a fever, and he's been sleeping off and on all day, which isn't like him because he's usually full of energy."

He could tell by the way her voice shook that she was worried, and as they made their way inside the small wood framed house he understood why. A young man who couldn't have been more than twelve years old stood just inside the doorway, holding on to the back of a tall chair. His unruly brown hair was plastered to his skin and his face was a deathly shade of white.

"William!" Miss Bowen exclaimed. "What are you doing up?"

He opened his mouth but no words came out, which alarmed Steven right away. He noticed how William swayed precariously on his feet, and he rushed over to keep him upright before he toppled to the floor.

"Your mom is right. We should get you back to bed."

When he put his arm around William's waist to keep him steady, his heart plummeted to his feet when he felt the intense heat emanating from William's body through his clothing.

"Miss Bowen, can you please bring me some ice wrapped in a bath cloth or dish towel? He's burning up with fever and we need to get it down as quickly as we can."

Tears cascaded down her face as she directed him to William's room before racing to the kitchen. Once William was lying comfortably on his bed, Steven opened his medical bag and removed a stethoscope and otoscope so he could listen to his chest and examine his ears and throat. Fortunately, his lungs sounded clear, but his ears and throat were extremely red and inflamed, which could explain the fever.

Miss Bowen returned with the ice and placed the towel against William's forehead. He opened his eyelids slightly and moaned, and Miss Bowen kissed his cheeks and caressed them gently with her fingers.

"It's okay, sweetheart. I know you're hurting, but Dr. Read is going to help you feel better. I promise."

He appreciated her show of confidence in him, especially since he was basically a stranger to her small town, and he smiled before continuing his examination. The lymph nodes in William's neck were swollen and tender, and although the ice brought his fever down somewhat, it still wasn't where Steven felt it needed to be.

"Miss Bowen, William's ears and throat are badly infected, and I would like to give him a shot of Rocephin, if it's alright with you. This medicine will take care of his fever more quickly than taking oral medication, and I'm worried if we don't get his fever down soon he might have a seizure."

As soon as Steven mentioned giving him a shot, William's eyelids flew open and he fervently shook his head while Miss Bowen struggled to keep him still. "No, no, no...I don't want a shot..." he mumbled.

Steven reached out and touched her hand. "Miss Bowen, I know how you feel about traditional medicine, and I understand because I was raised in an Amish household, but I promise I wouldn't recommend this if I didn't feel it was absolutely necessary."

The tears kept rolling down her cheeks, and the inner battle going on inside was more than evident by the pained look on her face. He felt guilty for suggesting something he knew was against her faith, but he had to do what he felt was right for William. Whether she decided to do it or not was totally up to her, but he feared there would be dire consequences if she refused. William's eyes swelled with tears, which only added to his misery, and he swallowed hard to try and keep it together. He dearly loved his job, but there were moments when he wished he'd never left home, and this was one of those times.

"Luke! Come here please!" Miss Bowen called.

Steven heard a door open in the hallway moments before a youngster appeared in the doorway. This child looked younger than

William by a couple of years, but they were almost identical with their wavy brown hair and blue eyes.

"What's wrong with brother?" he asked. His eyes were wide and expressive as he gazed at William, and Steven felt helpless and unsure of what to say. He'd tended to many children in his line of work, but having none of his own left him at a disadvantage sometimes.

"He's sick, and I need you to get Mr. Jonah right away. Do you understand?"

Without another word, Luke turned and bolted down the hallway and out the front door.

"Jonah Mills has been like a second father to my boys since my husband passed away last year," she explained. "Maybe he can help keep William calm while you give him the shot."

Steven thought for a moment. *Jonah Mills.* The name sounded vaguely familiar, and his spirits lifted when he remembered Bishop Abram introducing Jonah as Katherine's younger brother. He'd met dozens of people that Sunday in church, but Katherine was the only person he hadn't been able to stop thinking about, especially after Bishop Abram made it a point to mention to him that she wasn't married.

A few minutes later, Steven heard the front door open and he held his breath anxiously as heavy footsteps echoed down the hallway before Luke reappeared with Jonah by his side. They were both out of breath and Jonah's face paled when he saw William lying motionless on the bed. Steven leaned over and looked behind them, hoping that Katherine may have followed, but his hopes vanished when he realized it was just the two of them.

Jonah knelt by the bed and William's eyelids fluttered open when he heard him speak. "Hey, buddy. I got here as fast as I could."

Miss Bowen reciprocated the dishcloth between different spots on William's body, from his forehead to his cheeks and downward to his chest. "Dr. Read was just telling us how it would make William feel better if he gave him a shot to bring down his fever, but he doesn't like that idea very much."

Jonah nodded as if he understood before grabbing William's right hand and giving it a squeeze. "Our baseball game won't be the same next weekend if we don't have our best hitter there to help lead us to victory. I bet Dr. Read is great at giving shots. You probably won't even feel it."

He gave Steven a stern look, as if needing reassurance, so Steven reiterated to William that he would do his very best to make the shot as pain-free as possible. A couple of tears escaped and rolled down William's cheeks, but he ultimately agreed to it, and while Jonah, Luke, and Miss Bowen showered him with words of encouragement, Steven removed the bottle of Rocephin and a syringe from his medical bag and prepared the dosage.

Although it seemed to last an eternity, the amount of time it took between turning William over on his left side and Steven giving him the shot in his hip was mere seconds, and he was pleasantly surprised when William smiled at him when it was over.

"See? That wasn't so bad," Jonah said. "I'm really proud of you, buddy. You'll start feeling better in no time."

After Steven returned his supplies to his bag, he gestured for Miss Bowen to follow him into the hallway. While Luke took over holding the dishcloth to William's forehead, Jonah regaled him with jokes that had him laughing and smiling. When Steven saw the color return to William's cheeks, he breathed a huge sigh of relief.

"I'll come by tomorrow afternoon and check on him," Steven whispered, so they wouldn't be overheard. "Hopefully he'll be feeling a lot better and he won't have to take antibiotics, but we'll just play it by ear and see how he's doing."

Before Miss Bowen could reply, there was a knock on the front door, and Steven's heart skipped a beat when she opened it and he saw Katherine standing on the other side. Her long brown hair was pulled back and tied with a white ribbon at the base of her neck, and her cheeks were flushed a bright shade of pink.

"Is something wrong?" she asked, while trying to catch her breath. "I would have been here sooner, but I was getting dinner out of the oven when Luke came by, and all I heard was "William needs you" before he and Jonah took off running. I had no idea what was going on and I ran the whole way and..."

Miss Bowen raised a hand to stop her from staying anything else, which was probably a good thing, because she appeared on the verge of hyperventilating. When Miss Bowen ushered her inside and she caught sight of Steven standing in the living room, she flashed him a bashful smile. "Hello, Dr. Read. How are you?"

Steven felt tongue-tied at first, but he forced himself to say something – *anything*. "I'm doing good. Please...call me Steven."

Miss Bowen excused herself and returned to William's room, and suddenly the room became eerily quiet and very awkward. Katherine crossed her arms over her chest and rocked back and forth on her heels while Steven stuffed his hands inside his pants pockets and tried to come up with some topic of conversation.

Why was it so difficult talking to her? It wasn't as if he hadn't talked to other women before. It was ridiculous, really, and he felt embarrassed over his lack of wisdom when it came to the opposite sex.

"How is William doing?" she asked.

Steven cleared his throat before trusting himself to say anything coherent without tripping over his own tongue. "His throat and ears are badly infected, but I believe he's going to be okay. At first, he was afraid of getting a shot, but Jonah was able to talk him into it."

His comment made her smile, and Steven's heart fluttered. She was so beautiful, and her happiness lit up the entire room. He couldn't help but wonder if she even realized just how beautiful she was.

"Jonah is a lot older than William, but they are really close."

Katherine walked over to a chair in the living room and sat down, so Steven followed suit and took a seat on the sofa across from her. He could hear the muffled whispers streaming in the hallway, and his spirits lifted when he heard laughter coming from William's bedroom.

"Miss Bowen said he's become somewhat of a father figure since her husband died," he replied.

Katherine sat upright in her seat and flattened her palms on top of her knees. She looked uncomfortable, and he hoped it wasn't his presence that bothered her. If anything, he felt more at peace talking to her than he had since his arrival in Lancaster two months prior.

"*Yah*, I think it's good for them both. Our parents passed away three years ago, and there's only so much a sister knows about hunting, fishing, and farming. I do my fair share of it, but he needs more male friends in his life to talk to and spend time with."

Steven couldn't help but envy their closeness. When he didn't return home following his Rumspringa, he ruined any possibility of seeing or talking to his parents and two older brothers ever again. He didn't regret his decision to follow his dream of becoming a doctor, but he couldn't deny there were times when he wished he could go back and do things differently just to hear their voices one more time.

The sound of footsteps on the hardwood floor interrupted their conversation a few seconds before Jonah and Miss Bowen entered the living room.

"William is sleeping," she announced. "Thank you for coming so quickly, Dr. Read. He already seems to be feeling much better."

Steven took that as his cue to leave, even though it was the last thing he wanted to do. He would've been content just to sit and talk to Katherine all night. When he stood to go, she did the same, nearly causing them to bump into each other. They were so close he could see the tiny line of freckles that danced across the bridge of her nose.

"I should be going," he said. "I need to stop by the diner before they close."

Jonah waved a hand in the air, as if dismissing his comment. "Isabelle's Diner in Lancaster? No way. You can come to our house for a proper dinner. Katherine made her famous meatloaf and mashed potatoes."

He looked at Katherine, and he could tell by the bewildered expression on her face that she was shocked by her brother's suggestion. Because of that, he thought it would be best to politely decline, but before he had the opportunity, Katherine was agreeing with him. "I think that's a great idea."

He couldn't tell if she truly meant it or not, but he didn't want to be rude and ruin any chance he might have of seeing her again.

"Umm…okay," he replied, hesitantly. "Miss Bowen, I'll see you tomorrow afternoon, but if you need me before then, please don't hesitate to call me again."

She nodded before wishing them a good evening and leading them to the door. As Steven crossed the porch with Jonah and Katherine, he couldn't help but wonder what other surprises the rest of the night would hold.

* * * *

The following afternoon, while Jonah was busy gathering milk in the barn, Katherine took her cup of coffee to the back porch so she could enjoy a few minutes of peace and quiet. She also needed the coffee to keep her awake, since she'd gotten little sleep the night before. Although dinner ended early, she and Steven talked until midnight, and the remaining hours until daybreak were spent tossing and turning when she was unable to get him off her mind.

Katherine sighed contentedly as she recalled how easy it was to talk to him and the way his laughter reverberated off the walls in her tiny kitchen and wrapped around her heart. But despite the good that warmed her soul, there was also the hard truth that he'd been shunned from his own community when he didn't return from his Rumspringa.

He was now an English man who lived by English customs, and that was something she couldn't easily ignore, no matter how wildly her heart raced whenever he was near.

"What is causing such deep concentration, sister?"

Startled from her daydream, Katherine jumped and nearly spilled her full cup of coffee as Jonah laughed and bounded up the back-porch steps. When he sat down in the rocking chair beside her, she gave him a sideways glance without trying to hide her annoyance.

"I bet you were thinking about the new doctor in town," he joked. "Am I right?"

She didn't reply, but the blush in her cheeks must have given her away, as Jonah slapped his hand on the arm of the rocker and howled with laughter. "I knew it!"

Katherine steadied her cup of coffee on her lap and looked out across the large field behind their house. Rain clouds hovered in the distance and cast a shadow over the yard, but she didn't mind the impending rain. In fact, she welcomed it. If anything, it matched her solemn mood.

"I guess you think you're pretty clever, the way you snuck past me and invited him to eat dinner with us last night."

Jonah laughed again. "Oh, come on. You know you enjoyed it. I could hear the two of you talking and laughing from my bedroom."

Katherine sighed once again. "You're forgetting the circumstances, Jonah. Even if I wanted to be with Steven, it wouldn't be possible. He's already been shunned from our way of life, so no one would accept him."

Jonah frowned. "I don't think that's true. I know he and Bishop Abram are good friends, so there might be more hope than you realize."

Katherine took a sip of her coffee and let the heat from it sink into her bones. There was a lot to consider, but she was honestly afraid to get her hopes up and risk them being trampled on. There were also more important things to keep in mind besides her own feelings over the matter.

"I'm not going to leave you, Jonah. I made a promise to myself when mom and dad died that I would watch over you and take care of you – always."

From the corner of her eye, she caught Jonah turning in the rocker so he could face her, but she refused to look at him. She knew what would be behind those brown eyes, and she didn't want to see it. She'd lost count of the times they'd discussed their future and she didn't want to hear him proclaim again how he would be fine on his own someday. Perhaps he would when he found the right woman to settle down with, but until then he was her responsibility.

"Katherine, I love you, but you have *got* to accept the fact that I'm eighteen years old and a grown man."

Katherine cocked a weary eyebrow as she glanced in his direction. "I'm fully aware of that, Jonah."

He took off his hat and propped it on top of his knee. "There's no way I could ever properly thank you for everything you've done for me, but I want you to be happy. That's all I've ever wanted."

Katherine took another sip of her coffee. "But I am happy."

Jonah reached out and laid a hand on her arm, causing her to stop rocking and look his way. He had the sincerest expression on his face – something she wasn't used to seeing, since he spent most of his time cracking jokes and doing his best to make her laugh.

"I'm talking about the happiness I saw last night, Katherine. I didn't miss the way your eyes lit up when Steven was here, and I don't want you to risk losing that over me. Father taught me everything I need to know about running his business, and I can take care of myself and this farm."

Katherine let her eyes sweep over the property before she shook her head. "There's no way you can handle this all on your own."

Jonah's lips curled upward into a sly grin. "Who said I would be alone? I do plan on getting married someday, and I even have my heart set on someone special right now. I have for quite a while now."

Katherine sat up straight in her seat, nearly spilling her coffee again. "Really? Who is she?"

Jonah rested his head against the back of the rocking chair and grinned. "Don't even try and change the subject. We're talking about *you* – not me. You'll find out soon enough."

Katherine couldn't help but wonder who he was referring to, as she carefully considered every single woman in their community. There were several who came to mind, but she knew he wouldn't divulge his secret no matter how hard she pushed, so she decided to let it pass – at least for the time being.

"So, what do you think I should do?" she asked. "Should I talk to Bishop Abram first to see where he stands with us seeing each other?"

Jonah looked up at the tin roof and shook his head. "I think you should follow your heart. What do you *want* to do first?"

Katherine smiled. That was an easy question. "I want to talk to Steven and see if he feels the same way about me."

Jonah grabbed his hat and jumped to his feet. "That's what I was hoping you'd say. You should do that...*now*."

Katherine nearly choked on her coffee. "What? I didn't mean right this second."

Unfortunately, he wouldn't be swayed. Jonah took the coffee cup from her hand and disappeared inside the house. When he returned a couple of minutes later, the cup was nowhere to be seen and he had an umbrella hooked over his forearm.

"Take this in case it starts raining on your way to the phone."

He pulled Steven's business card from his shirt pocket and handed it to her, along with the umbrella. Katherine looked toward the dark clouds in the west and frowned. What if she didn't make it back before it started pouring rain? The phone shanty was a mile or so from their home, and the storm clouds were approaching fast.

Katherine stood up straight and squared her shoulders. No, it was now or never. If she kept waiting she would lose her nerve...and she would never hear the end of it from Jonah. Katherine opened the back door and grabbed her rubber boots, which were nestled in a corner just inside the doorway, and slipped them on before she changed her mind.

"Wish me luck!" she called to her brother, as she bounded off the back-porch steps and walked hurriedly toward the main dirt road. Her heart pounded furiously inside her chest, but it was a wonderful feeling – a mixture of excitement, anxiousness, and hope all rolled into one.

She prayed out loud as she walked, which bolstered her confidence. She refused to believe that God would bring Steven into her life only to break her heart by keeping them apart. With any luck, Bishop Abram and the others would be on their side as well.

* * * *

Steven unlocked his front door and retreated inside his house. He'd managed to get his groceries from the store to the car before the rain started, but now he had to carry them from the car to his house before the paper bags turned to mush and his groceries spilled all over the driveway. He groaned as the fumbled for the light switch. He didn't even own an umbrella.

Steven pulled his cell phone from his jacket pocket and plugged it into his charger on the kitchen counter. He'd noticed the voicemail icon blinking while driving home, but there wasn't enough battery life remaining to check it. He did see on the caller ID that it was the number to the Amish village, which was strange. He'd visited William Bowen around noon, and he was doing much better, so it couldn't be his mother calling.

At least, he hoped it wasn't. Steven's heart sank when he considered the possibility William may have relapsed. He quickly got the groceries inside as he waited for the battery to charge, and when he finished putting the items away, he saw a green light blinking on his phone, signaling that the battery was charged enough for him to check his messages. When he heard the voice on the other end of the line, he was taken by surprise.

"Hello, Steven. I…I've never left a message before, so I don't know if I'm doing this right or not. First off, I'm okay and there isn't an emergency. I apologize if I'm being too forward by calling you, but…I just wanted to let you know how much I enjoyed our conversation last night…"

His heart skipped a beat. *Katherine.* There was a long pause, but he could hear a loud noise in the background that sounded like thunder, and Steven frowned when he pictured her in the village's small phone shanty while the rain poured outside.

"I know our lives are very different, but…that hasn't stopped me from thinking about you. I really don't know what else to say other than I hope to see you again…soon."

Click.

Steven glanced at his wristwatch as he gathered up his cell phone and car keys. Going by the timestamp on his caller ID, fifteen minutes had passed since Katherine's call. As he raced to his vehicle, he silently prayed that the emotion he heard in her voice was the same as he'd felt since the day he met her. She was right about their paths in life being completely different, but he hoped that wouldn't stand in the way of something he felt in his heart could be very special. He'd grown up with the same Amish values and traditions, so there was no denying it could possibly be an uphill battle.

Steven roared the car to life and took off toward Katherine's house. The rain had died down to a drizzle, but the dirt road leading to the village was slippery and sent his wheels spinning. He took his foot off the accelerator and tapped his fingers impatiently against the steering wheel. He wanted to get to her as quickly as he could, but he also needed to get there in one piece.

As he neared Katherine's driveway, he caught sight of her walking across the front yard to her house. When his headlights shined upon her, he noticed how the small umbrella she carried did nothing more than protect her face from the rain. The rest of her was soaking wet.

Steven parked the car and took off on foot to meet her. She stopped when she saw him coming, and when he put his arm around her waist and led her toward the front porch, she didn't object. Just as he guessed, she was soaked to the skin and she shivered so much her teeth chattered. He opened the door and ushered her inside, and while Jonah went to the kitchen to get her something warm to drink, Steven grabbed a blanket from the sofa and draped it around her shoulders.

"What in the world were you thinking, Katherine?" he murmured. "You're going to catch your death of cold..."

She stopped him mid-sentence by placing a hand against his chest. "If you got my message then it was worth it."

Steven ran his fingers through her wet hair and moved it away from her neck, letting his fingertips glide softly against her neck. "I did."

Jonah returned with a steaming cup of coffee, but the moment he saw them huddled close together, he placed the cup on a table beside the sofa and excused himself from the room – but not before winking and grinning at them both.

Steven pulled the blanket tighter around Katherine's shoulders. "You should change clothes before you get sick...doctor's orders."

She laughed softly and the beautiful sound melted his heart and weakened his knees. When she took his hand, and led him toward the sofa, he followed like a love-struck teenager. Once they were seated, he picked up the coffee mug and encouraged her take a couple of sips. The color returned to her cheeks, although a bit slowly for his liking, and his first concern was getting some heat coursing through her veins.

"Steven...am I crazy for thinking this could turn into something more than just friendship?" she asked.

He squeezed her hands and moved closer. "No, I don't think that's crazy at all. I know we haven't known each other long, but I feel the same way. Do you remember me telling you last night how I wished I could go back and do things differently – how I never would have left my family?"

She nodded.

"I feel very strongly about that, and I know the odds may be stacked against me, but I really feel like Bishop Abram and the community will give me the opportunity to return to the fold when they see how I feel about you. All we do is pray over it and hope for the best."

When Katherine leaned into him and gently kissed his lips, he was caught off guard, but happily so. The moment may have been brief, but it left his heart racing wildly in his chest.

"We'll get through this together," she replied, emphatically.

Steven nodded – more certain in his conviction than ever before. He knew deep in his heart they were meant to be together...and he was ready and willing to do whatever it took to make that dream a reality.

9 798224 549481